THE *Lost* NOTE

Blessings Katie!

Eleanor Reed

ELEANOR J. REED

THE LOST NOTE
Copyright © 2016 by Eleanor J. Reed

Unless otherwise indicated, all scripture quotations are taken from the Holy Bible, King James Version, which is in the public domain. • Scripture quotations marked (NIV) are taken from the Holy Bible, NEW INTERNATIONAL VERSION®. Copyright © 1973, 1978, 1984, 2011 by Biblica, Inc. All rights reserved worldwide. Used by permission. NEW INTERNATIONAL VERSION® and NIV® are registered trademarks of Biblica, Inc. Use of either trademark for the offering of goods or services requires the prior written consent of Biblica US, Inc.

Printed in Canada

ISBN: 978-1-4866-1358-8

Word Alive Press
131 Cordite Road, Winnipeg, MB R3W 1S1
www.wordalivepress.ca

RECYCLED
Paper made from
recycled material
FSC® C103567

Library and Archives Canada Cataloguing in Publication

Reed, Eleanor J., author
     The lost note / Eleanor J. Reed.

Issued in print and electronic formats.
ISBN 978-1-4866-1358-8 (paperback).--ISBN 978-1-4866-1359-5 (html)

     I. Title.

PS8635.E353L67 2016   C813'.6   C2016-904178-6
                                               C2016-904179-4

Characters

HARRY JONES
HANNAH—Nursing Home Activity Director
JOANNE—Harry's niece
RYAN—Harry's great nephew
AMELIA—Harry's Red Cross homemaker
SAM—Harry's good neighbour
JEN—Hannah's daughter
JOHN—Jen's husband
TIM—Jen and John's son
JERRAD—Hannah's son
HOLLY—Jerrad's wife
MADDISON—Jerrad and Holly's daughter

1 BACHELOR
Harry

Bachelor Harry Jones, age sixty-four, kicked a few stones with his cane along the worn path following his morning chores on his south Saskatchewan farm. He rushed into his kitchen when he heard his phone ringing.

"Yes, this is Harry Jones speaking."

"Good morning, Harry. This is Hope Acres Retirement and Nursing Home in Elm Valley. We'll have a room available for you in our retirement home on August 15. Be sure to drop by and check out the details as soon as possible."

Harry was silent, and then managed to say a simple, "thank you." He carefully placed the phone back on the hook. It was the call he didn't want to receive. Harry put on the coffee and began making his breakfast. Just as he was about to make the toast, the phone rang again.

"Good morning, Uncle Harry; this is Joanne. Ryan and I are packing up and heading to our cottage for a week. Ryan will soon be getting ready to go back to school, and I'll be getting ready to teach my classes," Joanne added. "Oh, I guess you've already received the call from Hope Acres telling you that they'll have a room available for you on August 15. Don't worry, we will be over to see you before then to help you get ready for your move and to help with the plans for the auction."

Harry didn't respond.

"Bye for now, Uncle Harry; see you in a week or so," said Joanne.

"Goodbye, Joanne." Harry quietly hung up the receiver and walked slowly to his coffee table. He picked up his good old pipe—something he rarely did. As he gazed out the new bay window, he admired his wind-blown canola crop soon to be harvested on his one-hundred-acre farm, which was just a few miles from the town of Elm Valley. Losses began to pile up in his mind like the bales of canola that would soon be in the fields.

When Harry finally sat down to breakfast, his thoughts shifted to the family of four that came all the way from Ontario to check out his farm. He recalled the conversations with them about how much they liked his farmhouse with the big kitchen, the sun porch, and the large living room and dining area. This confirmed to him that they were the right ones to purchase his farm. They could hardly believe he recently put in the large bay window with the help of his neighbour. Their desire to leave busy Ontario to come to the wide open prairies, and especially to such a small community, touched a soft spot in Harry's heart.

The next few days seemed filled with news. Harry was still thinking about all that had taken place. The couple from Ontario phoned with word that the loan had gone through at the Elm Valley Credit Union, and the real estate agent called to ask his permission to put the SOLD sign on his property. Harry hesitantly discussed a closing date with the agent.

Harry's thoughts were interrupted by the barking of his dog, Collie. Sam Smith, Harry's good neighbour and best friend, parked his truck and came to the door.

"Good morning, Harry!"

"Come in, Sam. I'm a little late having my coffee today, but pull up a chair. You're probably ready for one, too," Harry welcomed him.

"Thanks. It looks like you've been a very busy man lately. I just saw your SOLD sign being put up, so thought I'd better get over to see you. I'm sure you'll need all the help you can get with the auction."

"You've got that right, Sam, but that's not all." As he brought the cream and sugar bowl and coffee mugs to the table, Harry said, "I got the call I never wanted to receive a few days ago. You know that new retirement home that my niece Joanne took me to a few months ago? Well, they phoned to say a room is available for me August 15. Sam, it's the call I never wanted to receive."

"This is unbelievable, Harry," Sam piped in.

"And that isn't all, Sam. Five minutes after that call, my phone rang again. This time it was my niece, Joanne. She just wanted to tell me how busy she was and that she'd received a call from Hope Acres saying that a room was coming available for me. She also mentioned that she and Ryan would be coming over to help me move and to get ready for the auction."

Sam carefully listened but didn't say a lot. "Did this niece of yours ever invite you to come and live with them?" he asked.

"No, that's not going to happen," Harry replied. "Joanne has been my Power of Attorney ever since my brother, Joe, passed away five years ago. My only sister, Jane, passed away a year later. Joanne is my only niece. I guess she thinks she can tell me what I need to do, and the doctor says I have to get off the farm."

Sam sat and sipped his coffee. "Harry," he finally said, "you've had so much to cope with lately. How would you like it if I picked you up some day soon and took you out for a coffee and lunch at that new Look Out Café in town?"

"That sounds great to me, Sam. Just make sure you don't make a mistake and walk into that new Hope Acres Retirement Home."

"No problem, Harry. How about Wednesday?"

"That would be just fine, as tomorrow my Red Cross homemaker will be here at 8:00 a.m."

"Thanks for the coffee, Harry. If I don't get home soon, my wife will be thinking I'm out for coffee and staying for lunch."

"Oh, I just thought of something, Sam. Remember you said you'd talk to me someday about the word *hope*. It just struck me today that if anyone needs hope right now, it's me."

"Harry, when we go to the restaurant and talk about your auction, we'll be sure to spend some time on that word *hope*."

"Thanks, Sam."

The afternoon seemed to go slowly. Harry found a note pad, so he started to take inventory and make lists. He thought he better at least do some planning for the auction before his niece showed up. As he prepared soup and a sandwich for supper, he did a lot of thinking about Sam's friendly visit. He wondered just what Sam would say about hope. He went over in his mind some of the dreams in his own life that had gone completely flat. *This is going to be a hard one*, he thought.

Sleep didn't come easily. Tomorrow he'd have to explain to Amelia, his homemaker, that he had sold the farm; he was sure it would be a long tea time this week after she finished her work for him. Then he thought about Collie, his dog and wonderful friend. He wondered what would become of him, as he wouldn't be able to take him to that new place. He knew one thing—Collie wouldn't be happy if he had to leave the farm. Then he pondered over his gardens, his chickens, and his favourite cow. He loved Molly's mossy breath. She would be the last cow to go. He felt grateful that he'd already sold the other cattle. And, oh, the auction sale … it will take hours to prepare all the details. Harry finally settled his thoughts; tomorrow would be another day.

2 *Collie*
TO THE RESCUE

Morning came early. It was a little before 8:00 a.m. when Harry headed out to the barn using his cane. His arthritis always felt worse early in the morning. As he stepped along the path to the barn, he imagined Amelia arriving. She had a definite routine: vacuuming, dusting, washing the kitchen floor, cleaning the bathroom, and sometimes making muffins. He fed the chickens and set out some food for Collie. As he was walking towards the water trough used for the cows, he tripped and fell over a small board. His cane went flying, and he couldn't get up.

"Oh, my arm!" he exclaimed. Harry's cane landed near his right side. *If I can just get a hold of it, I'll bang it on the trough*, he thought. He stretched out as far as he could and tried to reach his cane. Finally, he was able to put his two feet around the end of the cane and pull it towards him.

Bang! Bang!

He could see Molly and the other cows making quite a stir after he banged the cane on the trough. Collie soon appeared on the scene and grabbed Harry's jeans with his teeth. Harry hoped Amelia would come soon and find him. A thought came to him: *Why don't prairie farmers carry cell phones like a lot of the Mennonites do who don't have phones in their homes?* He'd seen them with their cell phones when he was in

Ontario years ago. He began to wonder if Amelia would check the time on the clock and worry about him.

Amelia did look at the time. Just as she was on her way to the barn, she saw a barking Collie run to her and then turn towards the barn. Amelia came rushing behind him, and he led her right to Harry.

"Harry, what are you doing? What happened?" Amelia gasped. "I looked at the time and wondered where you were, and then I hurried as fast as I could with Collie leading the way."

"I tripped on that stupid little board just as I got to the water trough to give the cows some water and feed," Harry quickly replied.

"Let me see if I can help," Amelia said, reaching down to help him.

"It's my left arm; I tried to get up by myself."

"Harry, I just can't seem to help you get up on your feet. I'll have to phone the fire department."

"The fire department! The whole town will know, and they'll think Bachelor Harry has really lost it."

"Sorry, but that's what I learned in my homemaker's course. They say if someone can't get out of a bathtub, and you know you can't help them, call the local fire department. Or, if they fall, don't try to pick them up off the floor," Amelia explained.

"Okay, Amelia, you'll find my barn phone just inside the door on the wall."

"It's okay, Harry, I have my cell phone in my uniform pocket," Amelia replied.

It wasn't long before the fire truck with two husky men in it came to the farm and found Harry in need. They got him up on his feet, being very careful not to hurt his arm any more than it already was.

"Could you take him right away to the hospital?" Amelia questioned. "I'll get my car and meet you there."

The firemen agreed to Amelia's plan.

"Amelia," Harry called out, "here's ten dollars and my health card. If you don't mind, could you pick up some milk and bread for me on your way back to the farm?"

"Sure, Harry, I'll take care of your health card and pick up your groceries. I want to know if you have any broken bones and what the doctor says for you to do. I'll have to report this to the Red Cross office."

"Thanks, Amelia. Don't you worry, now—I'll be just fine once I see the doctor."

Harry was right. The doctor told him that he was a lucky man. He didn't think Harry's arm was broken, but he sent him for X-rays just to be sure. It wasn't long until Harry was called back into the office. The doctor told him that the X-ray showed a slight sprain in the left arm. The doctor gave him a sling and encouraged him to wear it for a good two weeks.

"Harry," the doctor said, "I just have one question. Do you remember what I said a year ago about getting off that farm of yours?"

"Yes, Doctor. A family of four drove all the way from Ontario to look at it; it took them four days to get here. They loved my farm, and they got their bank loan approved this past week. I guess everyone will soon know since the SOLD sign went up yesterday."

"Good job, Harry! I'm very proud of you, and I wish you the very best in your retirement."

"Thank you, Dr. Cook, for those kind words and for helping me today."

A worker from the fire department came to the hospital and gave Harry a ride home. Amelia soon arrived back to her duties with the milk and bread. As she was opening the door, the phone rang. She reached for the phone and handed it to Harry.

"I just saw the fire truck coming from the farm," a panicked voice said. "Is everything okay? Was it a bad fire?"

"Yes, Alice, everything is okay," Harry replied. "I had a fall in the barn and needed a little help. Thanks for phoning. Bye for now."

Amelia put the kettle on right away and made Harry and herself a sandwich. "I guess you missed breakfast today, Harry. You must be very hungry."

Harry and his homemaker had a good visit over a cup of tea and the sandwiches. Harry, of course, told her all about his week. He knew she would be shocked to hear his news.

"Oh, Harry!" Amelia exclaimed. "I can't believe all this has happened in one week. With all of the government cutbacks, I sure will miss coming to see you twice a week. I may ask for the one day back, since you now have to wear the sling for a few days."

Just before Amelia left to go home, the phone rang again. Harry reached for it himself. It was Sam.

"Hi, Harry. We just got back from shopping and someone in the store told us they saw the fire truck going to your farm. Is everything okay? Did you really have a fire?" Sam questioned.

Harry assured his neighbour that there was no fire and that he just needed some help after falling in the barn.

"No broken bones, but I'm wearing a sling for a couple of weeks or so on my left arm," Harry assured Sam.

"Should we keep the same plans for tomorrow?" Sam asked.

"Sounds like a plan to me," Harry answered. "Thanks for checking on me, Sam; see you tomorrow around 10:00 a.m."

That night, Harry said a short prayer before he called it a day. "Thank you, God, for helping me today, and thank you that I don't have any major injuries from the fall."

3 HANNAH—A *Weekend* TO REMEMBER

Hannah Jansen arrived home from her day shift at Prairie Lane Retirement Home in Grove Hill, Manitoba. The telephone rang as she slammed her back door.

"Hannah, we didn't get time to talk after the big meeting when our shift was over," Joan said quickly.

"Thanks, Joan," Hannah said. An awkward silence followed.

"Everyone is so shocked," Joan added.

"You know how I love my job working with the staff and residents; it's my life," Hannah said in a quivering voice.

"I'm devastated, too, Hannah. It won't be the same without you at Prairie Lane. We'll all be lost without you as our Activity Director planning all those wonderful activities for the residents," Joan said.

Hannah grabbed a chair in her kitchen and sat down. "And we all know that without a union, there's not much anyone can do," she said. "I just hate it when the county does cutbacks in our community."

"Maybe after your mother's big eightieth birthday party this weekend, we can get together for a coffee after work. You'll still have a few weeks at your job, right?" Joan asked.

"Thanks, Joan. I'll still be there until June 15. If you have time to drop by tomorrow to greet my mom, that would be so special. Bye."

Hannah put the kettle on and took a coffee mug off the counter. Her to-do list was on the table in front of her. The first thing she stroked off was the white tent set up—done. She wondered how she would accomplish all that was on the list of things to get done and be ready for family coming on the weekend.

Tears streamed down her face. Exactly five years ago, Hannah's family and friends helped her celebrate her husband's retirement party. She remembered how the grandkids both sat on the miniature John Deere tractors and looked after the guest book. Nick kept telling them, "Good job!" He loved the grandkids. Hannah remembered three-year-old Maddison saying to Nick, "And we know a secret you don't know." His retirement party was close to his sixtieth birthday, so it turned into a surprise birthday party as well. What a celebration with over two hundred people!

Hannah walked slowly over to the counter and boiled the kettle again; this time she made a cup of tea. With her head bowed, she said a short prayer: "Heavenly Father, how can I do this tomorrow? Nick isn't here to help me. I know the family is coming, but I can't get my mind off his party just five years ago. I'm also thinking of my traumatic experience at work today. I'm so sad. You must know what I'm thinking, God ... Nick had a massive heart attack only three weeks after his big celebration. I want to thank You for how you're going to get me through this, and thanks for my family coming this weekend."

As Hannah closed her prayer, her elbows both on the table as she held her head in her hands, a Bible verse came to her mind: "*God is our refuge and strength, a very present help in trouble,*" (Psalm 46:1). Pastor Al had pointed out this verse to her a few years ago, and she remembered it. With tears streaming down her face, she said slowly, "Thank you, God, and thanks in advance for how You are going to somehow get me through this weekend. Amen."

As soon as she finished, a knock came on the door.

"Hi, Nana! We're here!"

"So soon!" Hannah said as she gave her granddaughter a big hug.

"Daddy got off early from work; he knew you'd need lots of help. Mom even brought supper for you in case you haven't taken time to eat."

"Thanks, Maddison; you go out and help your mom and dad carry in all your things."

Hannah rushed into the bathroom and splashed some water on her face and wiped her eyes. *That feels better*, she thought as she opened up the front door for her family, loaded down with overnight suitcases and decorations for the party for Grandma.

"Have you eaten yet, Mom?" Jerrad asked.

"Not really, Jerrad. I've been busy thinking about the party and everything we have to do."

"That's exactly what I thought. I made lasagna; it just needs to be heated up," Holly responded.

"We brought rolls, too, Nana," Maddison had to tell.

The family sat around the table and enjoyed the meal.

"Jen, John, and Tim will no doubt stop along the way for a bite to eat," Hannah said. "They should be here soon."

"Sure glad that we decided to come around this past week and put the big white tent up. It does look a little like rain this evening," Jerrad commented.

"Thanks to your neighbours, Connie and Dave, for all their help that evening with the tent," Holly added.

"Yes, I don't know what I'd do without them; they always seem to be helping me with something," Hannah expressed.

Hannah looked at her watch and couldn't believe it said 6:15 p.m. "Jen, John, and Tim should be here any minute now."

"Are you okay, Mom?" Holly asked.

"Yes and no," Hannah replied. "Maybe after we get some of the work done for tomorrow's big party, I'll get our family all together and tell you, but we need to get things done before it gets dark."

"Nana, I can't wait until Tim comes; you promised we could help decorate out in the big white tent. There they are now, Nana!" Maddison yelled as she watched the Dodge van turn into the driveway.

"Hi, Tim!" Maddison yelled as she saw Tim jump out of the car. "Nana says we can help with the decorations right now."

"Yeh!" Tim hollered back. "Mom packed the balloons in the big box."

Hannah soon helped the children get started on some decorating out in the tent. She had each of them make a HAPPY BIRTHDAY poster for their Grandma Molly's party. Jumbo markers and some photos helped them get busy with their creative project. She would get Jen and Holly to do the streamers a little later.

Hannah kept thinking about the day's events as she tried hard to keep the family busy. The Bible verses did encourage her as she gave leadership to the plans that evening. She whispered a quick prayer, "Thank you, Lord." Jen and Holly always enjoyed working together at family gatherings.

"All it would take is for Mom to see that big white tent again for her mind to go crazy thinking about it all," Jen added.

"But that's five years ago, Jen," Holly said. "There has to be something else."

Hannah was heading out to take more paper to the children when her cell phone rang.

"Hi, Hannah. I'm at Mom's right now helping her pack a little bag," Hannah's sister, Helen, said.

"That's great, Helen. I know you'll have her looking beautiful as always, sister," Hannah said before reminding her to arrive a bit before lunchtime the next day.

Hannah and Helen's mother was a retired teacher, and she so wanted one of her girls to be a teacher or a nurse. She doubled her wish. Hannah graduated as a registered nurse from a college of nursing in Manitoba, and Helen became a teacher and taught for several years.

As the family sat around the table Friday evening enjoying hot chocolate and snacks, Jen asked, "So, Mom, what's up?"

"Well, since you asked, here goes. We had a meeting after work today. Representatives of the county were there, along with the head staff. They informed us about raises and other issues. The last item on the agenda was about the cutbacks that the county has chosen to make. You won't believe this," Hannah exclaimed. "They cut my position as Activity Director at Prairie Lane Retirement Home. I'm through as of the middle of June."

"What?" John said as he jumped up from his chair. "That's unreal! What is the county thinking?"

"That's not fair," Jerrad spoke with a stern voice. "It was bad enough when they cut Dad's hours back on his grader job years ago, but not my mom's position. No way!"

"Sometimes they cut back a few hours ... but a whole position!" Jen said. "I'm so sorry, Mom." She rushed over and gave her mom a big hug. Holly also showed her concern with a big hug, too.

Hannah straightened her shoulders and wiped her tears. "Could someone check on the children in the playroom. See if they'd like more cookies."

"Sure, Mom," John said, as he was the one standing near the entrance to the playroom.

"So, I more or less crashed when I came home from work," Hannah explained as a tear rolled down her face. "I just got in the house, and a co-worker called. What would I do without those special co-workers?"

Everyone was quiet, and then Hannah continued. "Then to top it off, when I sat down to have a coffee and to look at my to-do list, all I could think of was my many memories of your dad's retirement and birthday party. Then you all know what came later that same summer."

Jen spoke first. "Mom, you've been strong for us all these years. Now it's our turn to be strong for you."

"You've got that right," John spoke firmly. "We'll all work together tomorrow to help you with Grandma Molly's eightieth."

The family agreed that they wouldn't talk about the job loss at Grandma Molly's party. The birthday party started at 2:00 p.m. in the Community Church. The grandkids looked after the guest book and enjoyed counting up the 150 guests that signed it. The church folk and many community friends enjoyed getting together; some commented that it was like "old home week." Grandma Molly received beautiful cards, and some people put little gifts on the guest of honour's table.

Balloons and streamers helped make it look festive. Hannah made a speech before they sang "Happy Birthday" to her mother. She thanked the Community Church ladies' group for all their help in preparing the sandwiches and setting up the hall for the occasion. Everyone applauded. Then Molly herself asked if she could say a few words. Helen came and stood beside her as she gave warm words of thanks for everyone who came, and a special big thank you to her family. She added, "Maddison and Tim, thanks for those posters you made and all the work you did, too."

The family gathered back at Hannah's home after the party, and she thanked each one for all their help in making her mom's party a success. Helen expressed her thanks to everyone, too.

"I had a wonderful party," Grandma Molly said, "and look at all the cards, flowers, and gifts I received."

"We had the most fun decorating the night before and helping with all those balloons, and we made sure we gathered up some to take home with us. Didn't we, Tim?" Maddison expressed.

Jerrad, Holly, and Maddison helped Aunt Helen get Grandma Molly all packed up with the flowers and gifts she received at her party.

"Thanks, Helen, for your big part—bringing our guest of honour!" Hannah expressed before they left for home.

After Jen and John had said good night and tucked Tim into bed, Jen and her mom talked about Hannah's situation.

"In the morning before we leave, I might check on the internet to see what jobs might be available for you to apply for in a retirement or nursing home facility."

Before Hannah headed for bed that night, she commented to herself, "This definitely will be a weekend to remember!"

4 HARRY'S DAY *Away* WITH SAM

Throughout the night, Harry could hear a gentle rain. He knew this would really perk up his tall sunflowers in the flower garden by his laneway. The chrysanthemums and roses would be healthier looking today … he felt sure of that. It was Wednesday, the day of his outing with Sam. At 7:00 a.m. he was off to the barn, wearing the sling on his left arm and doing his regular chores. He could feel the warm breezes of the Saskatchewan winds. The bright, blue skies would soon be breaking through after the rain. He stepped carefully along, using his cane and glancing at his flower beds from a distance.

He had a light breakfast, knowing he and Sam would be having coffee and lunch later in the new café in town. Then he took a quick shower and dressed up in his new navy shirt and dress pants. He quickly polished his black dress shoes. He knew his niece would be showing up in a few days, so he made sure he made a trip into town yesterday for a hair cut and some groceries. Two things she wouldn't have to tell him to do.

While he was waiting for Sam to come, he grabbed a notebook and a couple of pens, ready for the talk about the auction plans. He had already written other items in his book, like talking to the real estate agent about the closing date for the sale of the farm and the exact date when the new owners would move to Elm Valley. He wondered just how much more a person could handle in a few short weeks.

Sam drove into the lane a bit before 10:00 a.m., certain that Harry was ready for the day. Harry took along his light sand-coloured jacket, just in case it rained. He headed out the door and tucked his sling into his pocket, just in case he felt the need to wear it a little later.

"Good morning, Harry," Sam greeted him. "You're looking mighty fine for our day away. These town folk just love to see a nicely dressed up farmer with a neat hair cut and shave. It's going to be a great day away, Harry; I'm sure you feel you're ready for this."

"You've got that right, Sam," Harry said as they drove off in his fairly new black Ford truck.

As they were driving down the highway, they spotted a car stopped by the road not far from the farm.

"Looks like the tourists are out early today, taking photos of our wheat and canola crops, and no doubt the flower gardens. Don't forget, Sam, one of the main tourist attractions in our province is just two hours away."

They were near the restaurant and slowly drove by Hope Acres Retirement Home. Harry looked, but never spoke a word.

"Well, here we are. Finally getting to try out this new Look Out Café," Sam said.

Sam parked his truck in the huge parking lot. They both sauntered in, ready for a coffee.

"Good morning and welcome," the young waitress greeted them. She chose a table where they would have a good view. "Coffee for both of you?"

"Yes, thank you," they replied.

The restaurant was large with both booths and tables. The tables were adorned with attractive place mats featuring Saskatchewan flowers and points of interest to tourists. Harry and Sam could see the view of the valley from where they were sitting. The young waitress, Brianna, was quick to bring them a coffee and a menu.

"Since we're having a little meeting here today, if you don't mind, we'll just have a coffee now, and a little later, we'll be ordering off your lunch menu," Sam commented.

"No problem," said Brianna. "Feel free to stay as long as you like."

Some of the customers spoke to them as they walked by their booth. One neighbour who lived about three miles away, said, "Great to see you both! You can be sure I'll be at that auction of yours. We'll be watching the paper for the date. My son already has his eye on that good John Deere tractor and snowmobile."

"Thanks, Tom. I'll be looking for you," Harry replied.

"So, Harry, how are you feeling about all this—the auction, the move into the newly built nursing facility, and all the work ahead of you?" Sam asked.

"I always remember my father teaching me about taking one step at a time," Harry replied. "Lately, I feel it's at least two jumps at a time."

"Well, you've got your farm sold, and that didn't even drag on a long time. Then your doctor seemed very pleased with this recent news," Sam encouraged.

"And what an experience that was this week," Harry continued. "It was so embarrassing. And imagine Amelia having to find me on the barn floor. That was the most helpless feeling I've ever had. Sam, you know how I absolutely don't want to leave my farm. Sometimes I think it's just a dream. Me of all people having to make this change in my life, at age sixty-four. I know friends who are still hard at work, even in their eighties."

"It sounds to me like your doctor is really looking out for you; he wants you to have better health and many more years to enjoy," said Sam. "I'm sorry, Harry, I almost forgot to ask you how your left arm is."

"Thanks, Sam, for those encouraging words about the doctor. My arm is doing fairly well; I brought the sling along with me today just in case I need it," Harry explained.

Harry placed the small notebook on the table and tore out a few sheets for Sam in case he needed them. "I brought an extra pen along for you, Sam," he said.

"Thanks, Harry. Sounds like we're in business with these auction plans."

"First on my list is the date and time," said Harry. "I'm hoping I can book it for August 20 at 9:00 a.m. Auctioneer Sinclair is next on my list.

Sam, would you mind calling your auctioneer friend to see if he could do my sale that day?" Harry asked.

"How flexible are you if it can't be on the very day you've chosen?" Sam questioned.

"I only have one problem with that," Harry answered. "Joanne will be anxious about her classes starting soon, but it could be held a couple of days later. It doesn't have to be on a Saturday."

"I'll phone him as soon as I get home," Sam said.

The men talked over the list Harry had made that past week. It included everything from farm machinery to household furniture.

"That's a really good start on the list, Harry. After I talk to the auctioneer, he'll call you and set a date to come to your home to list everything that you have for sale. He always does a great job with the auctions," Sam explained.

"Joanne wants to help me, especially with the household items; this will be huge. I hardly know where to start."

Sam commented that he and his wife would be able to help in whatever way Harry needed. "I see the waitress coming our way," he said. "Brianna, could you let us have a look at your lunch menu? The time has gone by so quickly."

"No problem, gentlemen; I'll be right back." She handed them each a menu. "The special today is hot roast beef sandwich with fries and tossed salad."

When the waitress returned with two tall glasses of ice water, Sam ordered the roast beef special for both of them. As the men continued chatting, Harry wondered when Sam would have time to bring up the subject of hope. As they were waiting for their meal, he decided to speak up.

"I know you're a religious man, Sam; you attend the local church, and I've always looked up to you. I found myself using the word hope this week when I fell in the barn. I said, 'God, please send Amelia to the barn, and I really hope she'll come soon.'"

"Good for you, Harry. This is what faith and hope are all about. The Bible says that God is a very present help in time of need. Years ago, I found faith when I received the Lord Jesus as my personal

Saviour. I really like the words *faith* and *hope*. Hebrews 11:6 is one of my favourite scriptures," Sam shared. Sam also shared that recently he attended a community Bible study in town, where they talked about hope. "I copied a Bible verse that we studied. It reads like this: "*"For I know the plans I have for you," declares the Lord, "plans to prosper you and not to harm you, plans to give you hope and a future,"*" (Jeremiah 29:11, NIV).

"Thanks, Sam. I just knew you would be the one to ask about hope."

The waitress came along with the hot roast beef sandwiches. Sam offered a short prayer of thanks for the meal and their time together. As they enjoyed their meal, their conversation about hope continued.

"Well, I don't know if you can be of any help to me or not," Harry said. "If you don't mind," he continued, "I need to share a story that goes back over forty years ago. It happened at the time of my high school graduation. I wrote a note to a girl in my graduating class. I never got a reply, or even a phone call. I have absolutely no clue as to what happened to my note. Sam, all these years I've never forgotten about it. I call it my 'lost note.'"

"Do you know where she is now? Did she ever get married?" questioned Sam.

"All I can tell you is that the whole family moved away from Elm Valley."

"Thanks for sharing that, Harry. Just remember that verse I mentioned in Jeremiah about hope," Sam commented.

"Anyone for dessert today?" Brianna asked. "We have cherry and peach pie, plus apple crumble."

Sam piped up, "I'll have cherry—my favourite."

"And I'll have apple, please," Harry said.

"Would you like ice cream with your pie?"

"Yes, please," they both replied.

As they were enjoying their dessert, Harry realized that he'd never returned the call to Hope Acres to say when he would be in to check out his room and to pay his first month's rent.

"Sam, do you mind doing me a huge favour on our way home?"

"What is it, Harry?"

"I need to stop by that Hope Acres Retirement and Nursing Home to check out the room and talk to the lady at the desk. Now, that's only if you have time, Sam."

"No problem, Harry. I told Ellen we'd be away for the day."

As they went up to pay for the coffees and meal, Harry thanked Sam. "That will be one more of my jobs to stroke off my list if we can stop at Hope Acres."

The men left the waitress a good tip and thanked her for the delicious meal and dessert. Harry commented on the huge hanging baskets of chrysanthemums; there were pink, white, and red ones near the entrance to the Look Out Café.

They soon left the parking lot and drove into the visitors' parking lot at Hope Acres Retirement Home. Harry and Sam quickly noticed the Open House sign.

"No better time than today, Harry, to check this out. You take the lead, and I'll be right there with you," Sam added.

Sunflowers in tall vases graced the welcome table. Small bouquets of red and yellow roses were on the tables for visitors to enjoy while they were having juice and cookies.

"This looks quite inviting," Sam commented.

Harry stopped by the welcome desk with his cane in his hand. "Good afternoon. I'm Harry Jones from the Elm Valley area." With his right hand trembling a little, he placed both hands on the counter. "I received your phone call about three weeks ago saying there will be a room available on August 15."

The receptionist began checking out the name *Jones* in her registration book. "Yes, here you are," she said. "It looks like Room 121 is the one we have reserved for you. Let me call the Director of Nursing; she'll be with you shortly."

When Mrs. Agnew came to the desk, she offered to give the men a tour.

"This is my friend, Sam Smith; he very kindly came along with me today," Harry explained.

"Welcome to both of you," she said.

As they followed Mrs. Agnew, they saw many of the residents in wheelchairs or using walkers, and quite a few with canes. A few of the residents in wheelchairs had their heads leaning down and both hands folded on their trays. Others were being assisted by nurses to their rooms or to the tables for a drink of juice and a snack. Mrs. Agnew opened up Room 121 with her master key.

"This will be your room, Mr. Jones. We supply the bed, the dresser, and your clothes closet. You may bring your own bedspread or choose to use the ones that Hope Acres supplies. Also, bring a few pictures for the walls, and perhaps a nice chair and a desk for your room. Do you have any questions?" she asked.

"Does this facility take residents on outings?" Sam asked.

"Yes, we do have our regular volunteers and two staff workers to help with this, and we are very pleased to say that we just purchased a large van to use for taking the residents on their outings." Mrs. Agnew also explained that all of the residents receive a calendar of events for every month.

The Open House tour ended with checking out the dining rooms, large activity room, and the chapel.

"It looks like we're still waiting on your first payment for the rent of your room," Mrs. Agnew commented to Harry. "Also, do you have a personal Power of Attorney or next of kin?"

"Yes, I believe my niece filled out all those papers months ago. Her name is Joanne McIvor."

"Let me just check this out for you. Feel free to go and help yourselves to some juice and cookies over there by the main desk," Mrs. Agnew kindly told them.

A few minutes later, she came over to their table and said, "You're right, Mr. Jones; everything seems to be in place. We'll just wait now for your first payment."

Harry thanked Mrs. Agnew, and he and Sam left Hope Acres and headed back home in Sam's truck.

As they drove back to the farm, Harry didn't comment on Hope Acres. "I sure enjoyed our outing at the new Look Out Café," he said. "Thanks so much for all your help, Sam. Oh, before I go, do you mind if I have that little card where you wrote out that scripture on the word *hope?*"

Sam handed it to him. "I forgot to mention that the word *hope* in the Bible is a sure hope, not just a "hope so" type of hope. Actually, it's my favourite word in the Bible."

Before heading into his house, Harry checked on Collie and gave him some water and food. He relaxed for the rest of the evening, but his mind kept going over the day and the tour of the Hope Acres Retirement Home. Around 9:00 p.m., he slowly walked over to where his pipe was, picked it up, and brought it back to his chair, never lighting it. The hour passed by slowly. He decided he had to call Sam on the phone.

"Hello, Sam; sorry to call you so late. Just want to thank you again for the day, but I've changed my mind."

"About what?" Sam questioned.

"It's about Hope Acres Retirement Home. I'm not going there. I just don't want to, and I've made up my mind."

They talked for a short time until Harry said goodnight. Sam promised to call back in the morning.

5 HANNAH'S *Search*

Early Sunday morning, Hannah walked by the computer room.
"Jen," she said in a surprised voice, "you're up already? It's only 6 a.m."

"Good morning to you too, Mom. I'm just on the computer. I kept waking up throughout the night thinking about you. I wanted to get a good start on the day before we have to leave for home," Jen explained.

"And I can just imagine already what you're searching for," Hannah said as she stepped into the den.

"The bathroom's free now, Mom. Come back into the computer room when you're done; by then I'll have done some job researching for you."

"Sounds good to me, Jen. I'll try to be really quiet so we don't wake up John and Tim. Everyone will be so tired after Grandma's party yesterday," Hannah added.

In a few minutes, Hannah tapped on the closed door to the computer room. She felt a sense of relief that her mom's eightieth birthday celebration was over.

"Mom, you'll be surprised at what I've come up with," said Jen. "Are you ready for this? Look at this," Jen said as she clicked onto the website.

Hannah was shocked to see an advertisement for an Activity Director at a new nursing home in Elm Valley.

"Elm Valley! No way, Jen! It's been years since we've been back there. Remember, that's where I went to school before we moved to Manitoba," Hannah exclaimed as she looked over Jen's shoulders at the information on the computer.

"Let's check out the application form to see what they're asking you to fill in," Jen suggested with great delight as she helped her mom.

"I'm putting the coffee on, Jen; this is just too much for me to handle so early in the morning." Hannah was filled with anxiety as she walked to the kitchen and got out the toaster. Jen wasn't long running off an application form for her mom. Hannah always did like to have something in her hand before even thinking of sending an email and clicking "send," or mailing it in herself.

"Coffee's ready, Jen," Hannah said with a smile on her face.

"Thanks, Mom. I always enjoy these early coffees and visits with you. I just love it!" Jen added as she gave her mom a big hug.

While Hannah put a couple of slices of bread in the toaster and placed some jam and peanut butter on the table, Jen said, "I kind of like the idea of you moving back to Saskatchewan, even if we'd be in different parts of the province."

"Was there nothing much on the website for Manitoba regarding job postings for Activity Directors?" Hannah questioned.

"The ads for Manitoba are mainly requiring R.N.s and P.S.W.s, and also housekeeping and dietary staff," Jen replied as she enjoyed her early breakfast. "There were absolutely no positions requiring Activity Directors in Manitoba." Jen sipped on the coffee in front of her. "Thanks, Mom. So what do you think?" Jen asked as she heard some voices from the bedroom.

"What's all this talk I'm hearing from the kitchen?" John's voice echoed loudly from the guest bedroom.

Jen jumped up from her chair and rushed into the guest room. Tim was just waking up in the bunk bed when Jen heard John exclaimed, "Elm Valley! That's miles from us, Jen."

"The job description looks just like something Mom would enjoy doing," Jen replied to her husband, John, while he joined everyone in the kitchen. As Jen was returning to the table, Hannah quietly walked back into her bedroom. Jen walked over, tapped the door, and peeked in. Hannah was quietly praying. "You know the plans you have for me … plans to give me hope and a future. Show me your will, God. Amen."

Jen remembered her mom sharing Jeremiah 29:11 several months ago when she herself was going through a difficult time with her work. Tim wasn't long coming onto the scene.

"Good morning, Nana; that sure was a fun party yesterday for Grandma," he said as Hannah returned to the kitchen.

"You have that right, Tim. You and Maddison were such a great help. Thanks so much," Hannah expressed as she set out some cereal for Tim and John.

The Baker family needed to get packed up and drive back to Saskatchewan; their home was in a small town an hour from the Manitoba boarder. Hannah's mind was cluttered with loads of thoughts and questions. At the top of the list was her home in Manitoba, a major subject in even thinking of moving away.

As Jen was preparing some bacon and eggs for John and Tim, John commented that Jerrad had mentioned to him during the party yesterday something about applying for a new job. John looked at Hannah. "Did Jerrad say anything to you about a possible job he was thinking of applying for at the dealership here where Dad worked for years?"

"No, he certainly never mentioned it to me. With all those people dropping by, I'm sure he wouldn't get my attention too easily," Hannah replied. "What's this all about?"

"Well, he commented that his own job wasn't looking too promising for the future, and he's getting tired of that long drive to work near Brandon," John answered.

"I didn't even know the John Deere dealership was looking for help. It sure would be nice to have Jerrad and Holly closer to me," Hannah said with a smile. "And for the company to know his own father was a very good employee would certainly be a plus."

"How do you feel about that application form in your hand, Mom?" John asked. "I've often heard about people who move back to where they used to live."

"Actually, I do remember how well I enjoyed our small community of Elm Valley; it was hard for my sister and I to move to Manitoba years ago," Hannah expressed. "I am interested, but now that you tell me about the possibility of Jerrad, Holly, and Maddison moving closer to me, I have so many mixed feelings."

"God has promised guidance for you, Mom," Jen encouraged. "Don't forget the verses in Proverbs 3:5–6. You often bring it to my attention. It says, '*Trust in the Lord with all thine heart; and lean not unto thine own understanding. In all thy ways acknowledge Him, and He shall direct thy paths.*'"

"Yes, how well I know those verses, but thanks for the reminder, Jen," Hannah said.

Just as the family got the suitcases in the car and were saying their goodbyes, the telephone rang. Hannah ran to pick it up.

"Yes, Jerrad, we were just talking about you. So sorry you weren't able to stay over as well. I know you both had commitments for today. How did the church service go that you had to lead this morning?" Hannah inquired with her greetings.

"Thanks for asking, Mom; it went really well."

"Jerrad, I'll give you a call back in a few minutes," Hannah added quickly. "I have some news about me, too."

"Can't wait for your call, Mom," Jerrad replied.

6 WELCOME Calls

Jerrad was surprised by all the news his mom shared when she called him back after the family left for Saskatchewan that Sunday morning. She was equally surprised at Jerrad's news that he was applying for a position at John Deere in Manitoba. Hannah questioned her son about all the details and wondered how it would all come together. She promised to call Jerrad back if she received any news regarding her application to Hope Acres Retirement Home.

A whole week went by, and Hannah wondered if she would soon receive a call or email from Mrs. Agnew, the Director of Nursing at Hope Acres. It felt strange not going to work on her usual schedule. Even though she'd hit sixty-three just a week prior, she had a desire to do something else. She felt the need for a change. She was tired of people asking if she was going to retire.

On Friday morning Hannah's phone rang as she was heading out the door to go grocery shopping. She dropped her purse by the door and picked up the phone.

"Yes, this is Hannah."

"This is Mrs. Elaine Agnew from Hope Acres Retirement Home in Saskatchewan. We received your application for the position of Activity

Director. We would be very interested in having an interview with you, Hannah."

"Thanks, Mrs. Agnew. I'm finished at my job here in Manitoba and would be very pleased if I could come for an interview."

"Would July the tenth work for you at 2:30 p.m.?"

"My calendar looks clear for that date; I'd be very pleased to meet with you," Hannah replied.

Before Mrs. Agnew closed the conversation, she said, "Don't forget to bring your letter of reference from your place of employment. We'll need that."

"Yes, I definitely will bring that letter with me, and thank you kindly for this opportunity."

"Thanks, Hannah; we'll see you on the tenth."

Hannah made her way to the grocery store to do some shopping. As she was at the deli counter, she spied her friend, Joan, from a distance. She'd been wanting to tell her about this new position. It seemed so hard to meet with friends again after finishing her job at the end of June. Hannah walked to meet her as she saw her coming to the deli. They greeted each other with a hug.

"Joan, I don't believe this; I was just thinking that I need to give you a call and meet you for a coffee or lunch. What are you up to today?" Hannah asked.

"I got called in for an afternoon shift today," Joan replied.

"Would you have time to meet for a coffee after you finish your grocery shopping?" Hannah asked.

"I'd love to, Hannah," Joan quickly replied.

"What about that new Coffee Culture restaurant? I haven't been there yet," Hannah suggested.

"Would 11:30 be okay?" asked Joan.

"Sure! I'll meet you there at 11:30."

Hannah arrived at the restaurant first and saved Joan a seat in a booth. Joan soon arrived, and they were both amazed at all the great varieties of muffins, cinnamon rolls, and tempting desserts. They both went up to the counter and ordered a coffee and a muffin.

"So, Hannah, before you share your news, I have to tell you that

Prairie Lane Retirement Home really misses you at work. It's just not the same any more," Joan stated.

"I miss all of you as well," Hannah said. "So, the weekend of Mom's eightieth, Jen and John stayed over, and of course I had to share my upsetting news about my job," Hannah began. "I was proud of myself that I didn't tell them anything until preparations for the party were over. The family was totally shocked at my news," she added. "Early Sunday morning, Jen was on the computer checking out employment opportunities for me."

"Your daughter didn't waste any time, did she?" Joan commented.

"Even before the rest of her family woke up, Jen gave me the rundown on some jobs. She commented that there were no activity directors mentioned in the job ads, but lots of R.N.s, R.P.N.s, and P.S.W.s. These were all for Manitoba. In Saskatchewan, there was one ad that really interested me," Hannah shared.

"I had the feeling that you weren't ready for retirement yet," Joan commented. Joan got excited about Hannah's news.

"Do you remember me telling you that I spent most of my early days in a small town called Elm Valley in Saskatchewan?" Hannah asked.

"Yes, Hannah, I do recall you commenting that when you finished high school you moved to Manitoba to do your R.N. training, and then you met Nick," Joan remembered.

"Well, listen to this ... Jen showed me an ad for an Activity Director at Hope Acres Retirement and Nursing Home. They've already had their open house. The facility is located in Elm Valley, Saskatchewan."

"So, Hannah, did you apply?"

"Yes, I certainly did, and guess what?" Hannah quickly asked.

"I can guess this one," said Joan. "You have an interview booked already."

"You're right again, Joan! It's July 10 at 2:30 p.m."

"Congratulations to you, Hannah! This is great!" Joan was excited to hear the news. They both checked their watches.

"We might as well do lunch now; the time has gone by so quickly," Hannah said.

"I've decided already what I would like," Joan said. "Are you by any chance thinking of Coffee Culture's famous B.L.T.s?"

"Yes, I sure am."

"Me too," said Joan.

As they were enjoying their lunch, Joan spoke enthusiastically about Hannah's job opportunity.

"I'm really excited for you. If you need company travelling to Elm Valley on the tenth, please don't hesitate to call me. I'd even take a vacation day if it's not my day off to help you out."

As they went their separate ways after lunch, Hannah said to Joan, "Don't work too hard on your afternoon shift today, and please give my greetings to all the gals you work with."

"No problem, Hannah. I sure will do that."

As Hannah settled back in her home after the welcome phone calls and visit that day, she enjoyed a relaxing evening wondering what the days ahead would bring.

7 APARTMENT *Search*

The night was long. Many thoughts came to Harry's mind. He went over the dates on his calendar regarding the sale of his farm—July 5, his auction sale date, with an alternate date set for August 20, and then August 15, the date he'd enter Hope Acres Retirement Home. He was also thinking about his call to Sam, telling him that he'd changed his mind about moving to Hope Acres.

Daylight finally came after a sleepless night. After he showered and dressed, Harry felt good about the day. He grabbed his cane and placed his sling on his arm. It seemed to make his arm feel a little more comfortable … for awhile, anyway. And he knew he was following the doctor's orders. He cared for his chickens, and of course made sure that Collie got fed, too. As he took a little walk through the barn, he was reminded of the incident when he said a little prayer, hopeful that Amelia would come and find him. He wondered if God would be interested in helping him with some of his other requests that seemed urgent to him. He couldn't get the word *hope* out of his mind.

He fixed himself a quick breakfast, knowing that he didn't have time to waste. Sam soon phoned.

"No, I haven't had a change of heart about my decision," Harry answered firmly. "I'm just heading out to the café for breakfast and to check out the morning paper. I need to look for an apartment today."

"I'd be happy to meet you there, Harry."

"Thanks, Sam; if you have the time, that would be great."

Before he went out the door, a strange feeling came over him. Then he looked at the calendar. July 31 was coming all too soon. He took a deep breath. "How could I forget about my birthday on the thirty-first," he expressed out loud. With keys in his hand, he left the house and made sure the doors were locked. As he walked to his truck, he had a strange feeling that just wouldn't go away. *Could it mean that Joanne and Ryan might show up without phoning, as they usually do?* he asked himself.

As Harry drove his truck down the road to pick up the local newspaper, his heart seemed to take an extra beat. He felt the pressure of finding suitable housing and cancelling his room at Hope Acres. As Harry pulled into the parking lot of the Look Out Café, he saw Sam waiting for him in his truck. They strolled in together and found a booth and a friendly, busy waitress.

"Good morning, Harry and Sam. You two are out bright and early this morning. Coffee for both of you?" Carol asked.

"Yes, and you can add an order of toast and jam onto that. Thanks," replied Harry cheerfully. Harry noticed the pile of newspapers inside the door. He didn't lose any time in picking up the *Elm Valley Herald*. When he got seated again, Sam asked if he really was serious about getting his own place.

Harry broke out in a smile. "Yes, Sam, and it's urgent that I do this today if at all possible."

Carol wasn't long in bringing their order. "Harry, I heard you were soon moving into Hope Acres Retirement Home," she commented.

"When I checked it out, it looked more like a nursing home to me. Just seeing all those wheelchairs and walkers kind of changed my mind," Harry said. "You don't happen to know of any vacant apartments in the community, do you?"

"As a matter of fact, I do," Carol replied. "Have you checked out the three storey apartment building on Valley Boulevard? I just heard the other day that someone has to move out because of health issues; it would be worth your while to check it out," she added as she rushed to the next customer.

"Thanks for this very helpful information; we'll definitely check that apartment out today."

As Sam and Harry were enjoying their coffee, they checked out the advertisements in the local paper. "Here's one for you," Sam suggested. "This is what it says: *Apartment available. Prefer a senior. Pets allowed. Rent $400.00/month plus hydro. Phone: 306-233-2222.*"

"That sounds just perfect for me, Sam. I could even take Collie and not let the new owner keep him on the farm," Harry cheerfully commented. Harry took the bill and left the waitress a tip for both of them. "I owe you one," he said to Sam as he paid the bill.

"I have my cell phone in my pocket," Sam said. "Should we get right on this and check both these places out?"

Harry gladly agreed. "You jump in with me and just leave your truck parked here, Sam."

Valley Boulevard apartments was the first stop. Harry pressed the button for the superintendent. Soon a nicely dressed gentleman came and greeted them. Mr. Grey told them about the one vacant apartment.

"I want you to know, though, that we don't have elevators in our building; you'd have to take the stairs up to the third floor." He also explained that any buildings with four floors are required by law to have an elevator in the apartment building, but that his building only had three floors.

"With my worsening arthritis, I'm not sure I could handle these stairs, but I'm willing to give it a try," Harry replied.

Mr. Grey lead the way to Apartment 302 with Harry and Sam lagging behind.

"Are you okay, Harry?" Sam asked.

"I think I'll make it, Sam, but I'm getting a little short of breath."

When they reached third floor, Mr. Grey expressed to the gentlemen that he wouldn't request first and last months' rent if Harry decided to take the apartment. "Here it is, gentleman," he said when they finally arrived, "a one bedroom with a balcony. The fridge and stove are supplied."

"We'll let you know very soon," Harry said.

"If you decide to take this apartment, try to give me a call today; there are several other people also asking about it," the superintendent informed them.

"Thanks for showing us this apartment," Harry said as he and Sam took the stairs down to the main floor.

As the men made their way to the next appointment, Harry expressed his concern about the difficulty of the stairs, and Sam totally agreed. They decided to stop in at Harry's farm to check on something before viewing the second apartment.

"Oh no," Harry moaned when they arrived, "just what I didn't want to have happen!" His voice told it all. There in Harry's yard was a van. Niece Joanne and her son, Ryan, had come for their visit, unannounced. Ryan jumped out of the van.

"Happy birthday, Uncle Harry!"

"I know we're a day early for your birthday," Joanne added, "but we just had to come to see how you're getting along with all your plans. Ryan and I just thought we'd come for the weekend and help you celebrate."

"Well, Joanne, I was on a little outing with Sam, but I'll give him a lift back to where his truck is parked and be back home in a few minutes," Harry said with a lump in his throat.

"Guess our house hunting is over for today," Sam said in fun as they drove away. "Remember that chess game last week? You sure beat me on that last move."

"What's happening today is sure throwing my game plan out," Harry said without missing a beat. As Sam left the truck and walked over to his own, Harry rolled his window down and hollered for Sam to come back.

"Here's my last favour for today," he said. "Could you call that number for that second appointment we made and cancel it? It would be just one less worry for me."

"No problem, Harry. I have the paper with the phone number. And don't forget Jeremiah 29:11: 'For I know the plans I have for you …'"

"Thanks, Sam. And by the way, I didn't tell you, but I've been doing a little more praying and reading in my Bible lately. That word *hope* keeps popping up in the Scriptures. I'll never forget our day away, Sam."

"Thanks, Harry. I guess these are the plans God has for us today," Sam said as he left the parking lot to go home.

8 THE *Celebration*

Harry's thoughts raced as he drove back to the farm to meet his surprise company. He wondered if he'd left his house in order and if the sink was clear of yesterday's dishes. He knew Joanne had a key and would be making herself at home. He was glad that he'd remembered to do some grocery shopping before the stores closed on Saturday.

Ryan could hardly wait to see Uncle Harry's new Chevy truck drive up the lane and into his yard. "Here he is, Mom!" Ryan yelled as he saw his great uncle park his truck near the house. As Harry was getting out of his truck, Ryan ran to meet him. "I can't wait for you to see what I bought for your birthday, Uncle Harry."

Joanne was still getting suitcases out of her van. She'd already taken the grocery bags into the kitchen, as she knew some items had to be put in her uncle's fridge. As they neared the back door, Collie welcomed them with his loud barking.

"Hi, Collie," Ryan said. "I miss seeing you." He reached down and gave Collie a big hug.

"Where were you all morning, Uncle Harry?" Joanne inquired as she stepped into the kitchen.

"Oh, just out for coffee with Sam at the new café that opened a few weeks ago," Harry answered.

"We even drove up to Hope Acres Retirement Lodge and checked out how things were progressing there," Joanne continued. "Ryan and I brought a few goodies for a little birthday celebration. I know we're a day early," she said as she took the sandwiches and pickle tray out of the fridge.

"And we bought your favourite kind of birthday cake, Uncle Harry," Ryan said.

"Here, Ryan, you can place the birthday serviettes and plastic plates on the dining room table," Joanne politely instructed her son.

"Who are the extra plates for, Mom?" Ryan asked.

"Shh, Ryan; it's a surprise." There was a knock on the door, and Joanne knew who would be there. "You go to the door, Ryan."

"It's your neighbours, Uncle Harry," Ryan announced.

"Come in, folks, and make yourself at home," Joanne greeted the guests. Joanne invited them into the dining room and showed them where to have a seat.

"You didn't tell me anything about this, Harry, when we were driving around this morning," Sam said. He'd been quite surprised when his wife told him about the party when he returned from his outing with Harry.

"I didn't know either," Harry spoke up. "So much has happened to me lately, I almost forgot it was my birthday tomorrow."

Ten-year-old Ryan was asked to say a blessing for the luncheon, and then Joanne invited everyone to help themselves to the sandwiches, pickles, and juice.

"When can I bring in my surprise gift, Mom?" Ryan asked.

"Let's wait until after everyone has some cake and ice cream," Joanne answered.

Joanne brought out the cake with candles and set it in the middle of the dining room table. Sam's wife, Ellen, started off the singing of "Happy Birthday," and everyone joined in. Uncle Harry wasn't long blowing out the candles. Ryan helped his mom serve the cake and ice cream.

"Okay, Ryan, now you can go out to the van and bring in your surprise."

"Close your eyes, Uncle Harry; here's your surprise birthday gift from me," Ryan said.

"A bird! What in the world will I do with this, Ryan?' Harry asked.

"Well, Mom thought that since you're going to that retirement place, you'll need a little company. Hope Acres told us that if you didn't want the budgie right in your room, the cage could be set in the hallway right near Room 121."

"Have you thought of a name for this little creature?" Harry asked as he looked into the cage again.

"I was thinking of the name Perry. What do you think?" Ryan said.

"You definitely have put a lot of thought into this gift, Ryan. Don't you worry ... we'll find a spot for him. Thanks for the card you made for me, too. You're a very thoughtful young fellow," Harry expressed.

"You're very welcome, Uncle Harry," Ryan said.

Next Sam's wife, Ellen, presented Harry with their gift and card. Harry carefully opened the card and then the gift. "You always know that I like chocolates, and your homemade jam and pickles. Thanks so much to both of you," Harry said gratefully.

Then Joanne gave her uncle his birthday card. He opened it as she explained, "I didn't know what to give you, but when I went to check out Hope Acres Retirement Home, I decided to give you the first two months' payment on your room rent."

"Thanks, Joanne. I know I kept putting off getting that job done. You shouldn't have done this," Harry commented.

Before Ellen and Sam left the celebration, they thanked Joanne for the invitation and offered their help for the upcoming auction. As the guests were heading out the door, Harry's phone rang.

"This is your auctioneer, Sinclair," the voice on the other end said. "I just want to confirm that August 20 is perfect for me to do your sale. Would tomorrow morning be okay for me to drop by and go over some of the details with you?"

"Yes, that will be just fine," Harry agreed. "And since my niece is here for the weekend, this will work out well. I might even ask Sam and Ellen to drop in at that time, too, as they sure want to help plan this major job."

"That's great, Harry; I'll see you in the morning at 9:30 a.m.," said Sinclair.

As Harry and Joanne filled up some boxes to get a head start on the work for the auction, Harry was filled with mixed feelings as he thought over his day and all that took place, including his time with Sam earlier in the day and the celebration that evening.

9 AUCTION *Plans and* MOVING PLANS

Sinclair was surprised at how much work Harry had done in preparation for his visit. Harry credited Sam for his help on their day away together when they listed a lot of the items for the auction. Harry and Joanne were prepared with coffee, tea, and cookies when they gathered for their meeting the morning after Harry's birthday celebration. Joanne offered to take the advertisement information to the local printing office where the weekly *Elm Valley Herald* was published. The auctioneer asked Harry and Sam to find two or three men to help with holding up the items for him as he auctioned them off. Joanne was asked if she would be able to help with the book where all the items would be listed.

"I'll need more than one more person to help me," she replied. "I can't say I can commit myself all day, as I'm busy getting ready for the new school year."

"I can look after finding some assistants for that, Joanne," Harry offered.

Ellen offered to ask the Community Church if they'd like to have a food booth at the auction. Everyone said that this would be a great idea.

"Can I help Mom now with getting everyone either tea or coffee," Ryan asked. "I'm getting a little bored already."

Auctioneer Sinclair was very busy with his book work, listing all the items to be sold. "Don't forget, folks," he said, "we need a lot of these small house items put in boxes; they'll be sold as one large item."

The discussion and planning continued for quite some time. Before Sinclair left, Ryan asked him if he'd seen the gift he'd given to his uncle.

"No, Ryan," Sinclair answered, "I'll take a peek just before I head out to do another small auction this afternoon. I could quickly do that right now. I did notice the cage when I came in."

Harry remembered to remind Ryan to have a look at Perry. "Ryan, did you remember to check out Perry when you got up this morning?"

"Oh ... no, but during the night I did. I couldn't sleep for awhile, and I thought Perry might like a little company," Ryan said.

When Ryan walked over with the auctioneer to show him Perry, they saw that Perry was gone.

"Oh no, Mom," he cried, "I forgot to close the cage when I gave him just a little more water during the night. Now what will we do?" He had everyone looking all around the house for Perry.

"Now, let's just all calm down now; he won't be that far away," Harry said reassuringly. "I can't see how he could get outdoors; he won't be too far away."

"I'm so sorry, Mom; I hope we find him soon," Ryan said tearfully.

Harry encouraged everyone to be nice and quiet and look around. They thought they had looked everywhere. Ryan sat quietly for a while listening for bird sounds. Everyone seemed quiet with anxious thoughts. All of the sudden, Harry said, "Shh! Everyone be very still and quiet." Uncle Harry stepped quietly away from the table and spied Perry on top of his high buffet, sitting beside a small ornament. He just stood by the buffet and held out the palm of his hand, waiting until Perry flew down and landed on his shoulder. Harry then quietly walked over to the cage and shut it tightly after his new-found friend went back into it.

The auctioneer finally got a peek at Ryan's gift for his uncle. As he was leaving, he reminded everyone about the upcoming auction.

"Thanks for coming, Sinclair, and for all the work you helped us accomplish this morning; all the best to you as you do the auction this afternoon," Harry said.

Sam and Ellen were thankful that Perry was found safe and sound, and Harry and Joanne thanked them for coming over. Joanne now had her plan.

"After lunch, we'll go up to Hope Acres and inquire as to the possibility of Perry getting cared for by their housekeeping staff until Harry is all moved in," she said. Joanne made a phone call to the facility, hoping she would get Mrs. Elaine Agnew on the phone. Fortunately, Mrs. Agnew had dropped by Saturday morning, and Elaine had told her the situation.

"We'll have no housekeeping staff until Monday morning, but I'm sure they'll be able to take care of Harry Jones' budgie; I'll just need to confirm with them on Monday. Harry's room is empty right now, so if he wishes to bring items before he actually moves in, he's most welcome to," Mrs. Agnew offered.

Joanne thanked her kindly and said she would contact her on Monday to confirm that her Uncle Harry could bring his new budgie and that the cage would be close to his room. Later that afternoon, Joanne, Harry, and Ryan packed up the truck with various items. Harry told Joanne that he'd like to take his comfortable chair, his desk, and a few pictures for the wall. Harry also made sure that his games were packed: chess board set, crokinole board, and other games that he thought Ryan would enjoy when he came to visit. Lots of junk had to be thrown into a dumpster; it looked like none of his family members did this while they lived on the farm. Harry tried to not complain a lot, but it did bother him.

"What can I help you with?" Ryan asked Harry.

"Ryan, go upstairs and you'll find an old fashioned school desk," Harry said. "Take a box and throw everything in it that you think is no good. If you do a good job on this, the desk is yours."

Cleaning out the old desk didn't take too long, and when he was done he rushed back downstairs to tell his Uncle he'd cleaned it all out.

"I threw everything in a box except two items," he said. In Ryan's hand was a small Gideon Bible. "Here, Uncle Harry, this is for you. It even has your name inside the front cover. I also have in my hand something you should take to your new place. Look at this … it must be a photo of you and your sister and brother."

"Thank you so very much, Ryan. You found two treasures indeed. Since I have very few photos of my family, I will for sure take this photo to my new place. And now the old desk, which I treasured for years, is yours, Ryan."

"Thanks, Uncle. I sure will use this desk and may even take it home with me tomorrow; that way it won't get into that auction. Thanks very much for your gift to me today," Ryan said with a big smile.

"What chair are you actually thinking of taking, Uncle?" questioned Joanne.

"Well, I don't feel I have a very nice chair to take; I was thinking of perhaps buying one this coming week," Harry told Joanne.

"I was wondering about the same thing. It now looks like I'll be here all weekend and on Monday too, now that I see all the work there is to do," Joanne said.

"Well, Monday seems like the right day for me, Joanne. We hopefully can get Perry settled, and then we can take a drive in my truck to the furniture store," Harry commented.

Their final plan was to take the truck with the items already packed for Harry's room on Monday, and then they would do some shopping for a new chair. About 9:30 p.m., Harry called it a day. He felt much was accomplished regarding his auction plans and also his move on the fifteenth. He thought about the rescue of Perry and how thankful he was for both his young nephew and his new gift. He thought about the efforts he and Sam put into trying to find an apartment on the weekend, and how he had the feeling that his niece and nephew just might show up. *So much for that plan*, he thought, but he gave himself credit for at least trying.

10 HARRY'S *Shopping* SPREE

August 15 was coming very quickly, and Bachelor Harry had much to do before moving into Hope Acres Retirement Home. Just as he was overwhelmed at the thought of packing his clothes, buying some new ones, and getting rid of a lot of items, his phone rang.

"Hello, Harry. This is Amelia. Just wondering if you need some help this week. I'm free both Tuesday and Wednesday."

Harry told her that he planned on going on a shopping spree the next day, but both Tuesday and Wednesday would be great. "Thanks, Amelia," he said. "I was kind of thinking along that same line. I could use a little help with several things. I definitely can give you work for a couple of days, and the pay would be over twice as much as you would make with the Red Cross."

"Oh, Harry, this is great!" Amelia exclaimed. "I'll come at my usual time both Tuesday and Wednesday of this week."

"Thanks, Amelia. I appreciate your call this evening, and I'll look forward to seeing you on Tuesday morning."

Early Monday morning after Harry did his few chores on the farm, he decided he needed to drive into town and do some shopping. He took Collie along for the ride. He noticed in the weekly paper that the one and only clothing store in town had a big sale on, and he desperately needed some new clothes to take to that new place. He was pleasantly surprised to get the call from Amelia. As he thought about the money he made from his farm, he decided he wasn't going to be cheap about spending his money. Stopping at the bank would be his first job that Monday morning.

He drove into town in his brand new black Chev truck. Amelia's call gave him an extra stride in his step as he walked with his cane into the bank, leaving Collie in the truck. A sense of nervousness seemed to creep into his heart as he thought about the terrible task of moving.

"Good morning, Harry," the bank clerk, Maddie, said cheerfully. "I hear you're busy getting ready for your big move and the auction."

"Yes, Maddie, the days are coming all too quickly," Harry answered. He made his withdrawal for cash and made his way to the clothing store, leaving Collie safely in the truck with the front window down just a little.

As Harry walked into the Main Street Clothing Store, he was greeted by Zach, the salesman.

"Good morning, Mr. Jones," Zach smiled. "What brings you here today?"

"I need some new clothes before I make my big move," Harry explained. In his hand he had a list of all the items he needed. "Here's my list." The list included a new suit, shirts, socks, underwear, jeans, two new dress pants, a spring jacket, a house coat, and pajamas.

"Where are you moving to, Mr. Jones?" questioned the newly hired salesman.

"I'm moving off the farm and over to Hope Acres Retirement Home, which was built quite recently," Harry informed Zach.

"Come along, Harry," Zach encouraged. "You sure came on the right day. We have a big sale on. For sure we can meet all your needs."

"I'm sure the whole town knows that my farm is sold. It's sure quite a job making this big move," Harry added as he picked up items and placed them in the cart. Harry shopped as quickly as he could; he didn't even care about the amount of money he would spend.

"The big item I'd like to buy is a new suit. I'm kind of thinking of either grey or blue," Harry commented as he neared the racks of suits.

"Maybe you should check out that grey one right now; I have a feeling some of these suits at such a good sale price will go quite quickly today," Zach suggested.

"Do you mind just setting it aside right now? I'd kind of like to get these other items as quickly as I can," Harry said as he looked again at his list.

"Sure, I'll just hang the suit right over here for now," Zach informed him.

It had been years since Bachelor Harry had taken time to enjoy shopping in the big store, and he was delighted with the shopping cart they gave him to use. All of the sudden, Harry remembered that Collie was patiently waiting for him out in the truck. He pushed his cart towards the till and told the cashier he would be right back.

"I just need to check on my dog in my truck," he said as he rushed out of the clothing store. Harry wasn't long coming right back into the store. He rushed toward the salesman.

"Sir, my dog has disappeared! He isn't in my truck," he said anxiously.

"We'll help you, Harry. Give us a minute." Zach went to the back of the store and told Caleb, the store manager, what had happened. He came to the front and spoke with Harry.

"Harry, you and I have known each other over the many years you've lived on your farm. I'll go along with you in your truck," Caleb offered. "We'll drive around Elm Valley and look for Collie. If we can't find him, then we'll definitely call the sheriff or police."

"I sure appreciate your help, Caleb. I had my truck locked. I don't know how he could get out; the front window was just down a very little bit," Harry said anxiously.

"Let's check out that new Look Out Café," Caleb suggested. "I know I've seen you there with Collie. I used to notice what a patient dog he is, just waiting there tied up outside."

When they arrived at the restaurant, Harry carefully stepped out of his truck and inquired if they'd seen his dog. Then they drove around by the new Hope Acres Retirement Home. Harry said that he'd taken Collie there one day just to walk around outside the place.

"He just never leaves the truck if I take him for a ride and stop for a few minutes," he said to Caleb.

"Harry, let's drive up to your farm; you never know these days just what Collie might do. He knows something is going on," Caleb said.

"Sure," Harry quickly agreed. "We'll take a drive there right now, Caleb."

As they were driving towards the farm, Caleb shared that he'd had a dog once that disappeared, so he understood the awful feeling of missing your dog. When they reached the farm lane, Harry spotted Collie and shouted, "There he is!"

"This is the best news I've heard today," Caleb said with a big smile.

"You've got that right, Caleb!" Harry agreed. "Thank you ever so much for driving up here with me on such a very busy day at your store."

As Harry stepped carefully out of his truck, Collie came quickly to his side, jumping up and barking. He quickly put Collie in the back seat, and they headed back into town.

"Oh no," Harry said suddenly. "I just remembered that early this morning I'd opened up the back window of the truck to air it out." He immediately got out of the truck and made sure the window was closed.

"No problem, Harry," Caleb reassured him. "We all forget things sometimes. The good news is no one stole your dog. By the way, I enjoyed that ride in your very nice new truck."

Caleb and Harry returned to the clothing store with their good news. Harry took a few minutes to finish his purchases; the store clerk, Wendy, smiled as she rang in each item.

Zach rushed over to the till. "You better check out that suit jacket to see if it fits you, Harry," he said.

"Oh, I'd forgotten my biggest item. Thanks, I'll do that right now," replied Harry. "And I'll be back later to check out one of those spring jackets on sale," he added.

"If the pants are too long for you, bring them back and my seamstress will shorten them for you," Zach kindly offered.

"The grey suit jacket looks perfect on you," Caleb said as he glanced over at Harry, who was walking around the store.

"Good job, Harry, and thanks very much for coming in today. All the best now," Zach said.

Wendy added up all his purchases. "That will be a total of $495.50, sir."

Harry opened his wallet and carefully laid the exact amount of money on the counter.

"Thanks so much, Mr. Jones, and I do wish you all the best as you make the move to Hope Acres Retirement Home in a few days," Wendy expressed as Harry took all his shopping bags to the truck.

When Harry got home from his shopping spree, he put the kettle on and made himself a cup of tea and a ham sandwich. As he relaxed over his lunch hour, he got his pen and paper out and wrote down some jobs for Amelia. One job would be helping him get his new clothes organized to take to Hope Acres. Harry was encouraged with a note that Sam's wife put in his birthday card, which was sitting on his table: "Hope is a seed God plants in our hearts to remind us there are better things ahead." He read it over and over. He always enjoyed reading anything to do with gardening and planting. As he was relaxing after his lunch time, he said a short prayer.

"Thank you, God, for the seed of hope you're planting in my heart. Amen."

11 HOMEMAKER'S *Help*

Amelia was right on time as usual on Tuesday morning to give her client, Harry, a hand with jobs before his big move. As she knocked on the back door of Harry's farm home, Harry was right there to welcome her.

"Good morning, Amelia! It's so good to see you again," Harry said.

"Good morning to you too, Harry," Amelia said as she came into the kitchen with a couple of bags in her hand. "I thought that with all this work we have to do, maybe it would help if I brought lunch for both of us. You likely haven't had a taste of my cherry pie lately," Amelia said with a smile.

"How kind of you, Amelia! And, no, I haven't had a taste of your delicious cherry pie for quite a while. It's always been my favourite," Harry said.

Harry gave Amelia a list of things to do; she always liked a list when she did homemaking with the Red Cross. She started the wash, and right away noticed some new items.

"I guess you must have enjoyed a good shopping trip," she commented. "I see a lot of new items. Looks like you're getting well prepared for your move. Good job, Harry!"

"Yes, Amelia, I did have a very good shopping trip. I'll show you my new suit later."

Amelia wasn't long getting out the ironing board after the clothes got dry.

"Even new hangers, Harry!"

"Yes, and the old ones will be thrown out."

Amelia carefully put the new shirts on hangers and commented that they could be taken right up to the new facility. During their lunch time, they talked about the move. While they were both enjoying the cherry pie dessert, Amelia asked Harry how he was really feeling about all the changes.

"Well, I'm trying hard to have a better attitude. You know how I was with the news that my room would be ready on August 15—it was the call I never wanted to receive."

"Good for you, Harry! It's one of the most difficult things to do," Amelia said, knowing how her own parents struggled with a similar decision.

Amelia helped with a lot of jobs. At one point she asked Harry if they could take some of the clothes to the new facility.

"My room is all ready, so I see no reason why we couldn't," Harry said. "Let's put them in my truck and take a drive up to Hope Acres."

Soon they had the clothes in a garment bag, and the suitcase was already packed.

"Don't forget, Harry, you still have a few days before your auction," Amelia reminded him.

"Don't worry, I'll leave enough jeans and work shirts and other items in the drawers here, as I'll be going back and forth from my room to the farm to do some work for a few days yet."

Amelia helped Harry carry the clothing and the large suitcase out to the truck. They arrived at Hope Acres Retirement Home, and Harry went in to inquire at the desk if it would be okay for him to bring in some of his clothing. A pleasant staff worker greeted Harry.

"Could I help you, sir?" asked Rosemarie.

Harry asked about his clothing.

"Yes, by all means," she answered, "just bring in whatever you have and I'll see that your name is put on all the items."

Amelia helped Harry with all the suitcases and clothing. Within minutes they had unloaded the truck and taken Harry's belongings to his room.

"Thank you kindly for all your help," Harry said as they headed back to the farm home. It was getting near the supper hour.

"Amelia, do you have any plans for your evening meal?" Harry asked.

"No, I don't at the moment," she replied.

"Why don't we go out for a meal after all the work you had to do today?" Harry suggested.

"Sounds good to me, Harry, but do you mind if I go home and change my clothes; I don't like to go out with my uniform on. Were you thinking of the Hope Acres Café?" Amelia asked.

"Yes, Amelia, if that's alright with you. Would you like to meet me out there at 5:30 p.m.?" Harry asked.

"That would be fine with me; I'll see you out there." Amelia said.

The special that evening was roast beef. While they were waiting for their orders, Amelia commented on Hope Acres Retirement Home. "I think you'll like it there once you get into the routine of the facility, and you get your room looking comfortable," Amelia expressed.

"Yes, I think you're right," Harry commented.

"So, Harry, what have you planned for work for me to do tomorrow?" Amelia asked.

"I've already started a list; I think you might not want to come if I add any more to it," Harry laughed. "Joanne and Ryan came recently, and we got some clean up jobs done. Ryan was very pleased when I asked him to clean out an old writing desk. I told him if he did a good job at it, he could keep it. They took it home that night; that's one less item for the auction."

Both Harry and Amelia enjoyed their roast beef dinner and a cup of tea. Since they had a piece of the cherry pie at lunch, they decided they didn't need any dessert. Harry told Amelia about the meeting with the auctioneer and mentioned that Sam's wife offered to help get a food booth planned out.

"That's great that Ellen offered to do that; perhaps it's something I could help with that day. No doubt I'll be hearing about this soon," Amelia commented.

Harry picked up the bill and left a tip. Amelia thanked him for the delicious meal, and they both went their separate ways, grateful that they didn't have to make a meal when they got to their homes. Harry tried to have a relaxing evening, and he gathered some boxes to get organized for the next day.

12 THE *Interview*

H annah shared the good news about her upcoming interview with her family. That evening, Joan called.

"Hi, Hannah; it's Joan. I'm very sorry to have to disappoint you, but I won't be able to travel with you on the tenth of this month. I have an out of town doctor's appointment that same day. I was speaking with Fran. She's off that day and wants you to give her a call."

"Thanks, Joan. I totally understand, and I definitely will give Fran a call right away. A big thank you, though, for your support regarding my trip, and the fact you wanted to come along with me that day. All the best in your appointment," Hannah replied.

Hannah gave Fran a call later that day when she knew she would be home from work. "Hi, Fran. Just thought I'd give you a quick call. Joan gave me the good news that you might be able to come with me on the tenth when I go for my interview. That's wonderful if it works out for you."

"I would just love to travel along with you as you head to Elm Valley for your interview. Things seem to be moving very quickly for you; this is exciting," Fran enthused.

"Would you be able to come over after work on Wednesday this week? We could talk things over about our plans for the tenth," Hannah suggested.

"Yes, Hannah, I'd be happy to come after work on Wednesday this week," Fran replied.

That evening Hannah felt so happy about her chat with Fran, and she was looking forward to her little visit after work on Wednesday. She always did like making her to-do lists, so she made one to get organized for her trip in just a few days:

1. Make a copy of the letter of reference she received from Prairie Lane Nursing Home
2. Take map and work out the travel plan.
3. Phone her daughter and son
4. Take a special outfit to change into for the interview
5. Get gas and check out car

Hannah checked her watch frequently on Wednesday. She felt excited about her co-worker coming after work. She even baked cookies that morning and had the tea kettle on to make Fran a cup of tea.

Hannah greeted Fran when she arrived, and they chatted about how things were going at Prairie Lane.

"The residents are still asking when you're coming back," Fran shared. "Everyone says it's just not the same without you there; they seem to be inviting more groups in now for entertainment, and they're also showing the residents more videos."

As Fran and Hannah were enjoying the freshly made cookies and tea, Hannah explained her plans for the trip. She said that Elm Valley was an hour and a half from the Manitoba border. As they would be making two or three stops along the way, she asked Fran to be ready at 8:30 a.m.

"Sure, Hannah, no problem. I'll certainly be ready then. What time is your interview?"

"My appointment is at 2:30 p.m."

The day of the interview came quickly. Hannah picked Fran up and off they drove to Saskatchewan. They stopped at Tim Horton's for a coffee and snack along the way. As they were driving along on the nice summer day, they both mentioned that it had been a long time since either of them had been to an interview. Hannah wondered if Mrs. Agnew would be asking her what type of activities she might be thinking of for this newly built facility.

"Maybe you can help me with this, Fran. Since I'm driving, could you just jot down a few ideas for me, just in case I don't come up with any ideas?"

"Since I work a lot of day shifts," Fran said, "I do remember some very creative ones. As you know, we have very limited time to help with this along with all the work that has to be done every day."

Fran mentioned the Hawaiian party, and how the lady residents looked so pretty with coloured leis around their necks, and flowers in their hair.

"I think you had fun at the dollar store buying a lot of items you needed," Fran mentioned. "The few volunteers we did have were invited to dress up, too, and to enjoy the noon luncheon."

Hannah added that one of the male residents said that the best part was the food. Small groups of residents really enjoyed making strawberry freezer jam. This was a great event, and later it was a little fundraiser for the residents. This was where the staff and the volunteers were an excellent help.

"Hannah," Fran said, "you always had so many creative ideas. Remember the Christmas events, the homemade Christmas cards, the little boxes, and the decorations for the tree? Some of the residents enjoyed making snowmen with a large pop bottle, cotton batting, and a Styrofoam ball for the head. Then they would decorate a little craft hat and other items for their snowman. Also, when you played basketball with those in wheelchairs; this was fun for them in the large auditorium." Fran wrote the ideas on the piece of paper to give to Hannah.

"Oh, there's a sign for Elm Valley," Hannah announced. "Twenty-five kilometres from here."

"I'll watch for that restaurant when we get into the town," Fran offered. "I remember that you planned to stop there and kill some time before your interview."

Hannah began to feel a little nervous as she thought about her interview.

"We'll take a drive through town first to find the home, and then we'll look for the newly opened café. We'll spend some time there before my interview. Does that sound like a good plan for us, Fran?"

"Yes, Hannah, that sounds wonderful to me," Fran replied.

It didn't take long for Hannah to find the newly built facility.

"It's not far at all from the restaurant we're looking for," she said. "We'll stop there now; it's time we took a break, anyway."

They both checked the menu out and decided to order a coffee and a sandwich. On the way home, they would stop for an evening meal.

"I can't believe we're here," Hannah said. "It's so nice to have you along with me, Fran."

After lunch, Hannah changed into her pretty blue dress and dress shoes and headed up to Hope Acres for her interview. Fran picked up a town newspaper and took her book along to read while Hannah was busy with Mrs. Agnew. Hannah parked in the large parking lot, and she and Fran walked together to the newly built building.

"It's the countdown now," Hannah said with a deep breath.

They walked into the main entrance. A friendly lady who had "Hilda" on her name tag greeted them. She called on the phone to the D.O.N.'s office.

"Hannah Jensen from Manitoba is here for her interview this afternoon," Hilda informed Mrs. Jensen.

"Bring Hannah down to my office," Mrs. Jensen replied. "I can start her interview right away."

"Your friend can come along with you, Hannah," said Hilda. "There's a very nice lounge right by the D.O.N.'s office; you can wait there for Hannah."

"Thanks, Hilda; that's very kind of you," Fran said.

Mrs. Agnew greeted Hannah with a handshake and welcomed her to Hope Acres Retirement Home. "After your interview," she said, "we'll invite your friend to join us for a tour of our new facility. So, Hannah, you've come quite a distance, and I understand Elm Valley was your hometown many years ago. I'm sure you'll notice many changes."

"Yes," Hannah replied, "but I'm sure I'll run into people I knew long ago, and some things in small towns just never change."

Mrs. Agnew had Hannah's application and resume on her desk in front of her. She asked her a few questions, and Hannah mentioned her job as an R.N. in a hospital for the first few years of her working life.

She was interested to know about Hannah's family, and she asked a few questions about her work at Prairie Lane Nursing Home.

"I loved my work at the nursing home, and I worked there for ten years. I so miss working with the residents there, and of course all the staff members. I remembered to bring my letter of reference with me; I'll give this to you right now," Hannah said as she handed her letter to Mrs. Agnew.

"Thanks, Hannah; I'll be sure to take this to my staff and board meeting in a few days."

Mrs. Agnew read the letter quickly and commented that it was a very good letter.

"Hannah, the old facility was quite well staffed, but like most homes, we had to keep adding more nursing staff. We just never did have a good volunteer program. Perhaps you'll be a great help along this line. Let me ask you to briefly tell me about some of the activities you might suggest that you were familiar with in your position in Manitoba."

"First of all," Hannah began, "let me tell you that I am very keen on a volunteer program for this job; we never felt we had enough volunteers. I have a few ideas to suggest a little later concerning this, but back to your question about activities. These are just a few I can think of right now. A Hawaiian party with volunteers invited to help, along with any staff who have some time available. At my former job, we helped dress up the lady residents with flowers in their hair and a few creative things we bought from the dollar store. We also made Christmas crafts, cards, and gift tag tickets from old cards. Making strawberry freezer jam was a big hit; we had enough volunteers to make this very successful. The residents used the items we made for a fundraiser in which the staff had an opportunity to purchase a small jar. The volunteers were very excited and helped with many of our special activity days. We had a huge box of dress up clothes and Halloween items, too.; hats were really a big hit, I might add. Of course we did birthday celebrations and special teas.

"It sounds like you had lots of fun doing all this, and I'm sure you could tell me so many more ideas," Mrs. Agnew commented. "Hannah, do you have any questions?"

"I'm just wondering how many residents live in your new facility? And does Hope Acres have a van for taking residents out for short tours and other kinds of outings?" Hannah asked.

"Yes, and by the way, you can just call me Elaine. Right now there are a hundred and thirty residents, and we just purchased a new van in the month of June."

"That's great; the residents seem to enjoy the outings, don't they?" responded Hannah.

"If you have any further questions, perhaps I can even answer them as I give you and your friend a tour of our new facility," Elaine suggested. "We're so pleased with this new building, as our old one didn't have nearly enough space, or even a large enough room to handle a large crowd. I might add that we just learned this week that the old facility is going to be renovated into senior apartments. This will be great for some of our residents who feel they can handle living in an apartment. Our facility would be near by if they need more assistance."

Elaine and Hannah walked toward the lounge, and Hannah introduced Elaine to Fran. Mrs. Agnew took them to see the three levels of care locations. First she showed them the residential care area, then two other units, and then the two locked-in areas, one for the ladies and one for the male residents. She took them to see the whirlpool room, the large, multi-purpose auditorium, the chapel, the various lounge areas, and the dining rooms.

"Wow!" Hannah exclaimed. "This building is wonderful! I love the wide halls and the nicely painted walls."

"I wish Prairie Lane Nursing Home had this much room," Fran said. "It sure is a very nice facility." Fran thanked Mrs. Agnew for the great tour.

Mrs. Agnew said her goodbyes to Hannah and her friend, and Hannah thanked her for the interview and the tour.

"Thank you for coming all this way," Elaine said, "and you and your friend have a great trip back to Manitoba."

Hannah and Fran went to their car in the parking lot and headed towards home. First, though, they just took a drive around town to see the streets and any houses that might be marked "For Sale." There were a few.

"While I was waiting for you," Frain said, "I read the whole local Elm Valley newspaper. It contains real estate ads, cottages for rent, and other properties. You'll have to have a look at this when you get home, Hannah."

They drove quite a distance before they stopped for supper. Hannah was tired.

"I've so enjoyed having you for company today, Fran. You've been very helpful. Now I just have to wait for the results of my interview. I feel in my heart that I did alright."

While at McDonald's for a meal, they chatted about their experience at Hope Acres.

"Well, she did ask the question about activities," Hannah shared, "and my little paper on which you wrote down some ideas came in handy."

When they arrived back home, Fran said her goodbyes to Hannah and wished her all the best. They were too tired to do any more travelling that day. Hannah thanked Fran again for her company and for their nice visit together along the way. They both felt that it was a fun time and were so thankful how everything worked out.

Hannah decided to give her family a call in the morning to tell them about her experience and her safe trip to Elm Valley and back home again.

13 HARRY'S *In*

Harry was allowed to move into Hope Acres Retirement facility a few days early. It suddenly hit him that he forgot to mention to the staff that he wanted to get his phone connected in his room and he wanted the same phone number he had on the farm. Harry had so much on his mind. The fact that the new family wasn't moving in until a week after the auction meant that he had to spend some time still caring for Collie, and maybe even the chickens.

"Good morning, Mr. Jones," greeted Pat, one of the staff members on duty. "Let me help you with your big suitcase; you lead the way, and I'll get the door for you. I believe you're the new resident booked for Room 121." Pat made him feel at home.

"Thank you kindly," Harry said.

"Is there anything we can help you with this morning while you settle in?" Pat asked.

"Yes, there is. Could you get someone to come to my room to help me get my phone connected; I'd like to keep the same number as on the farm. Then when the new people move in, they can get their own phone number. I have a lot of calls to make before the auction next week, and since I'm going back and forth to the farm during the day, I need to be able to use the phone at the farm home."

"Yes, Harry, I'll call the business manager of our building right away. His name is Orville; we call him O.J. I'll ask him to come to your room, so I would ask that you just stay in your room at this time. I know he'll come shortly to assist you and connect with SaskTel as well," Pat informed him.

After he talked with the business manager, Harry went back to the farm to attend to a few necessary things. He knew Mrs. Agnew wanted to see him around 9:30 a.m., so he hurried back to his new home. He pulled into the driveway of Hope Acres and was surprised to see his dog.

"Collie! What are you doing here?"

Collie's leash was left in the truck, so Harry was able to fasten the leash securely on a post nearby. Harry walked into the building and stopped by Mrs. Agnew's office.

"Do have a chair, Harry," she greeted him. "This won't take too much of your time. Once you finish the registration procedure, there is a book you must sign whenever you leave the building. We need to know the time you leave and the time you return. We are very responsible to families and just need to know when you come and go. I'll show you the book when we are through with our chat."

"One problem I know I'm going to have is with my dog," Harry said. "He seems to want to follow me wherever I decide to go. The plan is for him to stay with the new owners when they arrive a week after the auction."

"I understand fully," Mrs. Agnew replied. "When I took on this job, I had a dog. Just like your dog, he wanted to always be by my side. Here is a calendar of events you can keep in your room; you'll find a bulletin board on your wall. Put your calendar on there; you'll receive a new one each month. You may choose whatever events you wish to attend."

Harry thanked her as she walked with him to the front entrance where she showed him the sign- in book. Since he was heading right back to the farm at this time, she had him sign his name and the time he was leaving the building. He took Collie off the leash and put him back in the truck. As he drove back to his farm, he wondered just how he would adjust to the routines, and having to sign in and out each time he left the building and returned.

Sam had noticed that Harry left early for the Hope Acres facility that morning. As he and Ellen were heading out to shop, they called in on Harry, as they noticed his truck was back in his yard.

"Good morning, neighbour," Sam said as he drove up by Harry's farmhouse. Harry was just letting Collie out of the truck. "Did you get through all the routines at Hope Acres already?"

"Not really, Sam. I had to have a talk with the director of nursing, and I was able to talk to the business manager regarding my telephone hook up. I was glad to get that settled. Sam, I have a major question to ask you. How much would you charge me if I asked you to take Collie off my hands until I at least get settled into Hope Acres. I know I'll be going back and forth between now and the auction, and I need to at least get into a bit of a routine. I need to sleep there at night and go for my meals in their dining room."

Sam wasn't long giving his answer. "Harry, you know that we've been good neighbours for years now on the farm. I don't have a problem looking after Collie until the new owners arrive. I remember you telling me that they really wanted to have your permission to keep Collie on the farm; he wouldn't feel at home anywhere else. Harry, back to your question. There will absolutely be no charge to do this for you. Right now, Ellen and I are going to town to get stocked up on some groceries. How would it be if I stopped back in after we are through shopping? We need to get this settled and organized very soon regarding Collie."

"Sure, Sam, that will be just fine. I have a few things on my list to do. One important thing is to call the Jackson family and tell them the actual time of the auction, and to ask them some questions," Harry stated.

Later that day, Harry reached the Jacksons in Ontario. "Good morning, Mr. Jackson! How are things in Ontario today? This is Harry Jones calling."

"Just call me Fred. How are things there in Saskatchewan?" Fred asked.

"Everything is going fairly well. I just want to remind you that my auction will be on August 20 and starts at 9:00 a.m."

"Thanks, Harry. Our plans are to be in your area at that time. Are there any other questions you have for us regarding your farm?" Fred asked.

"Yes, another reason why I'm calling is that I can't remember if you said you were interested in me leaving my chickens here on the farm. Actually, I just moved into the retirement home this morning, but I could get my good neighbour to care for them until you come. I understand you are quite interested in having my dog, Collie, remain on the farm This is my wish, too. I just need to confirm this plan with you."

"Yes, Harry, for sure, we'd love to have your wonderful Collie remain with us, and your chickens, too, if that is still alright with you," Fred confirmed.

"Thanks Fred; this means so much to me," Harry replied.

"I have one main question to ask you, Harry," Fred said. "As you already know, we have sold our home, and the new buyers want to be in by August 24. We've rented a cottage for a week not too far from your area. Our truck with our furniture will be arriving August 25. Is this okay with you?"

"Yes, this plan is quite alright with me; I'll make a note of this date on my calendar," Harry replied.

"Thanks, Harry, for your call; this confirms a lot of things for both of us," Fred said.

Harry returned to Hope Acres in time for lunch. As he went to the dining room, he remembered that he hadn't signed back in. He took his cane and went back to the book to mark his time of return, and then he returned to the dining room to have his meal. The feeling of not wanting to ever make this major move was now a reality. Harry was in!

14 Hannah's *Good News* and House Hunting

On Wednesday morning, Hannah was busy doing some housework when the telephone rang.

"Good morning, Hannah. This is Elaine Agnew from Hope Acres Retirement and Nursing Home in Elm Valley, Saskatchewan."

"Good morning to you, Mrs. Agnew."

"Hannah, we had our meeting earlier this week, and we would really like you to take the position of Activity Director at Hope Acres. We feel that all of your experience in this field would be a great asset to our new facility," Mrs. Agnew continued. "If you're still interested in this position, we'd like you to begin on August 10."

"Thanks so much for this very welcome call, Mrs. Agnew," Hannah said. "Yes, I'm still very interested in this position. Since it's summer time, I may decide to just rent a cottage for the month of August while I look for a permanent place to live."

"I'm sure your family will be a great help in checking places out for you on the computer, and the *Elm Valley Herald* will also be a great resource," Mrs. Agnew suggested.

"Thank you, Mrs. Agnew. On the day of my interview, I bought a copy of your weekly town paper at that time. I certainly will check that out again soon. Thanks so much for this wonderful opportunity; I look forward to seeing you soon," Hannah stated with assurance.

"Take care, Hannah; give me a call if I can be of further help to you," Mrs. Agnew offered.

Hannah sat down and had her second cup of coffee. She did some deep thinking and jotted down the phone calls she would have to make. First, though, she whispered, "Thank you, Lord." Her first calls were to her son, Jerrad, in Manitoba, and her daughter, Jen, in Saskatchewan.

"Mom, this is wonderful news," Jerrad said. "Congratulations! We don't have many days to help find you a place to live; we definitely will check this out really soon, Mom." Hannah thought the world of her twins, Jen and Jerrad. They often thought the same way about issues. She called Jen next.

"Mom, this is the best news ever!" Jen said excitedly. "Congratulations on getting that new position in Elm Valley. We'll talk again real soon … like today, okay?"

Hannah picked up her Bible and said a short prayer. One of her special verses was Proverbs 3:5–6: "*Trust in the Lord with all thine heart; and lean not unto thine own understanding. In all thy ways, acknowledge him, and he shall direct thy paths.*"

Jen wasn't long working things out. She got permission from her boss to leave work on Friday noon, and also from Tim's teacher for him to miss some school. She knew her mom would need family this weekend with her new position beginning in just three weeks' time. Her husband, John, was working out of town all week.

Jen called her mom back. "Hi, Mom. I feel that I needed to get a few hours off on Friday and drive to Manitoba to spend the weekend with you. John is working out of town. I have already called him on his cell. He's okay with everything, and so happy about your news. If it's okay with you, Tim and I will travel Friday afternoon. That way we can be with you on the weekend."

"I'm not sure if I can handle all this good news. Thank you, Jen! This is wonderful to think you have worked all this out so soon," Hannah said.

"We'll call Jerrad and Holly when I get to your place. Perhaps we could all plan to go to Elm Valley on Saturday. Now don't you worry ... we will be there for you. Remember, we promised you this at Grandma Molly's party," Jen assured her mom.

"Thanks, Jen. I'll look for you and Tim on Friday."

Hannah gave a quick call to Holly to give her a heads up on just what was happening, and to tell her that Jen and Tim were coming on Friday.

"I'll give Jerrad a call at work to tell him to keep Saturday free; I just know he'll want to see you too," Holly said. "We're very excited about you getting the good news about your new position; congratulations from all of us."

Friday afternoon wasn't long coming. Hannah had just come back from getting a few groceries. She knew Jen and Tim would definitely be staying all night with her. Tim came rushing to his Nana's door; he knocked and walked in.

"Good to see you, Nana," he greeted her and then gave her a big hug. "Mom is bringing in a few things from the car," Tim said.

Hannah put the kettle on, as she knew Jen would be ready for a cup of tea. She set out some juice and cookies for Tim.

"So, how have you been, Mom, since you got that excellent phone call from Hope Acres Nursing Home?" Jen asked.

"I'm still excited about the call. You just never know when you apply for a job how many other people are wanting the position. I feel honoured that they accepted me, that's for sure."

"Since this is Friday afternoon and the time is going by quickly," Jen said, "I feel that I should help you with a few phone calls about housing before you plan supper."

"Thanks, Jen. I did save the *Elm Valley Herald*, which I picked up from my trip when I went for my interview. This might be a good start," Hannah told her daughter.

Jen quickly wrote down some numbers as her mom quickly looked at the Real Estate section of the paper. Then Jen made the first call regarding a cottage in the tourist area about twenty-five kilometres from the town of Elm Valley.

"Sorry, we just rented out this cottage to a family who had a house fire recently in Elm Valley area," the representative said. "No doubt others will soon be coming up near the close of summer."

"Jen, I really would like to be able to find something closer and not have to move twice. The bad weather will come late fall," Hannah expressed.

"Let's try this one. It's a two-bedroom house for sale; it's listed under Star Real Estate. Their office is right in Elm Valley," Jen said.

"Okay, I'll give this number a call," Hannah said. "Sometimes in small communities the houses are cheaper than in the cities, for sure. This one is listed at $49,000.00"

The staff secretary answered the phone. "Could I ask who's calling?"

"This is Hannah Jansen calling from Manitoba. I'm interested in the ad I saw in the *Elm Valley Herald* over a week ago now. It's the house right in your town and listed at $49,000.00."

"Yes, I know the one you mean. This house is in very good condition. We've had several offers. The owner turned down all the offers so far," the secretary told Hannah.

Hannah told the secretary that the family would work out plans that day as to when they could go to Elm Valley.

"The broker would be pleased if you would like to make appointment, even on the weekend. I definitely will tell him that you called," the secretary pleasantly said.

"Well, this is a very good start, Mom. We know that homes for sale are not that plentiful, especially in a small town. I think moving to a cottage would be your last resort. I'd rather see you buy a home." Jen just knew this would be best for her mom.

Hannah called Jerrad right away on his cell phone.

"I'm just leaving for home shortly. Is anything wrong, Mom?" he asked.

"No, nothing is wrong, Jerrad. Jen is here, and we've made a few calls regarding housing. We need you and Holly to consider making a trip to Elm Valley tomorrow. Give us a call back and we'll explain things in more detail," Hannah told Jerrad.

"No problem, Mom. I knew something like this might take place quite soon," Jerrad added.

Jerrad's call came around 6:00 p.m., just when Jen, Tim, and Hannah finished their supper. Jen talked to her twin brother and told him about the calls. Jerrad said that he and his family would definitely help them the next day. Hannah took the phone. "Jerrad, if we made an appointment with Star Real Estate for 1:15 p.m. Saturday, would this be okay with you and the family?"

"Yes, for sure, Mom. We need to get on that right away. We'll talk about time and travels later," Jerrad said. His mom felt reassured with the plans.

All the necessary calls were made. Jen and Tim would take Hannah to Jerrad and Holly's home, which was an hour's drive from where Hannah lived. Jen's husband, John, also made his plans to meet them at the real estate office on Saturday.

Saturday arrived and it seemed like a family reunion when they all got together and met at Star Real Estate office. They were all excited to see the house that was for sale in Elm Valley. It was quite attractive looking, with one bedroom on the main floor and the other one in the newly renovated basement. It had a very nice kitchen and medium size living room. There was a den off the kitchen. The basement looked quite spacious. The family talked privately later with real estate agent and made an offer.

Since a lot of people didn't put in a high enough offer, Hannah decided to actually offer the asking price, as housing was so limited in the small community. The real estate broker, Paul, said he would get the papers prepared and give the owner a call that evening.

"Could you come back in an hour, Hannah, with your family? This would give me time to do some of the paperwork and call the owner," Paul suggested.

The family all gathered at the Look Out Café and got a cold drink or coffee. They were all happy with the house. They chatted about a lot of things, and soon it was almost time to meet back at Star Real Estate Office. Jerrad's cell phone rang just as they were standing up and about to leave the restaurant. He sat down again and took the call.

"Hello, Jerrad. This is the John Deere Company in Manitoba. We're so sorry to be so long in getting back to you. We want you to know we are gladly accepting your resume, and the fact that your father worked here is a plus. The new position is available in a couple of weeks' time," the secretary of John Deere told Jerrad. "Are you still interested in this position?"

"I can give you my answer right now," Jerrad replied. "I'm very pleased to receive this call, and I can work things out to begin at that time. Right now I'm in Saskatchewan and have a family matter to settle. We're heading back to Manitoba this evening. I'll give your office a call when I get back home. Thanks for this very important call you gave me today."

Hannah's family couldn't wait until Jerrad got off the phone to see what this message was all about. They all had smiles and were talking at once.

"This is great timing," Jerrad said as he clicked off his cell phone. Now all of you will know that I got the job at John Deere."

The family all piled into Hannah's van and drove to the Star Real Estate office.

"Now we'll see if there's also good news there," Jen said as she stepped along quickly.

The real state broker greeted them with a smile. "Well, I have good news for you! The owner readily accepted your offer, of course, and was very pleased."

The family expressed their appreciation and thanked him kindly. Then Hannah and Jerrad went into the office to discuss the financial part of this major transaction. Maddison and Tim had a good idea.

"Hey, everybody," said Tim, trying to get everyone's attention in the car. "Maddison and I want go back to that new Look Out Café in town; we're both getting hungry and bored."

"Now, that's not a bad idea, Tim," his dad replied. "Can anyone guess what our topic of conversation might be?"

Tim answered quickly. "I know, Dad; it will be about Nana's house hunting and Uncle Jerrad's cell phone call."

"There isn't much more exciting than this today, that's for sure," Holly spoke up as she took her place next to Maddison and Tim.

They weren't long parking their car at the Look Out Café. The children ran on ahead of everyone and couldn't wait to get back into the restaurant for the second time that day. The family all enjoyed their meal, and the other guests in the restaurant were probably wondering what kind of a celebration they were enjoying. Brianna, the waitress, seemed to be enjoying these out of town visitors. Hannah was sure she would be meeting her again when she moved to Elm Valley very soon.

As everyone was returning to their cars, each one received a big hug and words of grateful appreciation from Hannah. Soon they were on the road heading for home. Jen and Tim stayed over until Sunday morning and then left for their home in Saskatchewan. John had his own vehicle, as he'd come from his workplace to join the family in Elm Valley.

As Hannah relaxed on the Sunday after a major weekend of house hunting and all that went with those travels, she felt a calm feeling knowing that she had found a home to purchase. Now Jerrad knew that he was welcome to rent her home. She knew Jerrad would be calling her this week to make arrangements for a visit to discuss the moving plans.

When Hannah told her Pastor Al her plans to move shortly, he shared a couple of verses from Psalm 37:4–5. She had written them down on a piece of paper in the front of her Bible. Before she headed to bed, she read them again: *"Delight thyself also in the Lord: and he shall give thee the desires of thine heart. Commit thy way to the Lord; trust also in him; and he shall bring it to pass."* Hannah whispered a prayer of gratitude to God, thanking Him for the excellent day and the answers to prayer, and especially for her success in house hunting and for Jerrad's new job.

15 *Looking* FOR HARRY

The week before the Jacksons from Ontario moved into the farm home, Harry was quite comfortable in his new place. He'd been trying to clear everything up since the auction and was still going back and forth to his farm. Joanne and Ryan decided to take a trip to the farm to pick up the last few items they bought at the auction. Ryan was excited to see his Uncle Harry in his room and to know how Perry was getting along. He hoped that the housekeeping staff and Uncle Harry were taking good care of Perry.

The family decided to let Ryan stay with Uncle Harry for a visit while they spent time on the farm. There was always so much cleaning up to do after an auction. They had to take care of the dumpster and also lots of garbage. When they arrived at Hope Acres and went to Harry's room, he was not there. Perry looked quite content in his cage and quite healthy.

"I don't know where he'd be," Joanne commented to Ted. "I'm so very worried about romance."

"Don't be crazy, Joanne," Ted replied. "He's too old for that."

"I have an idea," Ryan piped up.

"What's your idea, Ryan?" his dad asked.

"Well, don't forget Uncle Harry sure likes that new Look Out Café in town. Maybe we should take a drive to see if we can find him there."

"You go and wait in Uncle Harry's room," Joanne told Ryan. "Your dad and I will check with the head nurse on duty this evening."

Joanne and her husband walked to different areas looking for a nurse and keeping an eye out for Uncle Harry. They finally found a nurse.

"Let me see," Nurse Angela said, "we'll look at the book where residents sign out if they are leaving the building. No, it doesn't look like he signed out. I have a better idea; let me find out from the dietary staff if he was here for lunch today." Angela headed into the staff kitchen area.

"Yes, Harry Jones was here at lunch time," one of the dietary staff stated.

"Mom, why don't you phone Uncle Harry before we leave home," Ryan suggested. "Now that he's in a new place, you never know just where he will be."

"Good idea, son. You'd think I would have learned this after all the times we just wondered where Uncle Harry would be on the days we came to visit him," Joanne said in an annoyed voice.

Just as they were ready to give up and leave, they saw some residents going into the café by the chapel area. Ryan dashed on ahead and went into the café.

"Mom, Dad," he yelled, "Uncle Harry's right in here. It looks like he's having a cup of tea."

"Well, Uncle Harry, we finally found you! This is such a big facility; we never realized this café was even here," exclaimed Joanne.

"Hi, Joanne. I know you've met Amelia, my Red Cross homemaker, on several occasions. She's hoping to be one of the volunteers at Hope Acres, and she dropped by to pick up a form and to have a cup of tea with me," Harry told the family.

"Hello, Joanne," Amelia greeted. "Let me get you a cup of tea, or if you prefer, there is also orange or apple juice. And how about a cookie? It's all free. The residents really like this café where they can have a guest and a nice visit together. There are other snacks and fruit, too."

"Uncle Harry, we're wondering if Ryan could stay with you for awhile this afternoon. Ted and I are cleaning up things on the farm, so it will look good when the new owners come," Joanne said.

"Sure, Joanne. I'm not planning on going anywhere this afternoon. I'd love to have Ryan stay here while you're down at the farm," Harry replied.

Joanne and her husband left and thanked Amelia for the tea, juice, and snacks. Amelia walked with Harry and Ryan to Harry's room. She said her goodbyes and promised to call Harry soon.

Ryan made himself at home in his uncle's new place and asked him all about Perry and how he was liking his new home.

"Well, Ryan, tell me how your summer holidays are going. You'll soon be back in school." Uncle Harry was always interested in Ryan.

"That's right, Uncle Harry. I was hoping I could come for a visit soon with you, but Mom just decided today on short notice that they would come over to see how you are doing and go down to the farm. Uncle Harry, do you like Amelia? Have you ever had a girlfriend? I hope you really like Amelia; I sure like her."

"My, you ask a lot of questions for a young lad," Harry laughed. "I would say a definite yes to your first question. She's been my Red Cross homemaker for several years; she's a wonderful lady. Amelia likes to come and visit me in my new place. I take her to the café for a cup of tea sometimes, but she just likes the orange juice."

"Oh, I just thought of another question," Ryan said. "Has Amelia ever been married?"

"Yes, but about ten years ago her husband took very ill and passed away," Ryan's uncle told him.

"Well, I guess I won't ask any more questions; I don't like sad answers," Ryan said. "I understand you're doing just fine with Perry. I hope he never gets lost again like he did that night on the farm. I'll never forget that, as it would have been my fault if anything bad happened to him that night."

"Well, Ryan, because I'm so busy running back and forth to my farm lately, I've allowed the housekeeping staff to keep caring for Perry. Some day soon I'll give the department some money for helping me out. So, you still haven't answered my questions. How are your summer holidays going?"

"Well, just last week a friend invited me to go to the Community Church Vacation Bible School. We played games. There was a craft time each day, and contests for attendance and learning some Bible verses. It was a lot of fun, and we had snack time, too; I loved that part. The parents were invited to a special closing on the last day," Ryan shared.

"I'm very pleased that you were able to attend the week of Vacation Bible School. My neighbour, Sam, attends the Community Church in town," Uncle Harry commented.

"Uncle, remember the other day when you asked me to clean out the old school-type desk, and then I told you that I found a treasure."

"Yes, Ryan, and I was very pleased you found my Gideon New Testament and also the photo. If I told you how many years ago I received the little Bible, you'd likely think I am old. I know you were very pleased when I told you that the desk was yours," Uncle Harry said.

"Yes, and I already have it in my bedroom and will start using it very soon. I'm very proud to have this gift from you," Ryan told his uncle.

"You know, Ryan, I was never much of a church person, but these past few months I've been reading my Bible. Now that you've found my little Bible that the Gideons gave me years ago, I've been checking out those pages at the back. Before I headed to bed one night this past week, I actually signed my name at the back, and I said a prayer to our Heavenly Father, thanking Him for the gift of salvation. I finally found a peace, hope, and happiness in my life that I've been trying to find for a long time."

"Well, Uncle Harry, I too signed the back of my Gideon Bible this past week at Vacation Bible School. We got points for bringing a Bible each day," Ryan continued to share. "Pastor Phil from the Elm Valley Community Church came one day and briefly explained some scripture verses to all the boys and girls. He said his favourite verses are John 3:16 and I John 5:13. He also was in charge of telling a missionary story three times this week; he made the stories really interesting and had us laughing a lot. So, Uncle, tell me what you're finding to do here in your new Hope Acres building," Ryan asked.

"Since this new Activity Director came, we have lots to do. See my calendar on my bulletin board? If you even glance at it, you'll know I'm sure not bored here like I thought I'd be. Before I came here, Sam and I played chess pretty well once a week. He'll be up this coming week to have a game with me. We have games and activities at least twice a month, and I'll probably be helping some of these residents play crokinole. Too bad you couldn't come some day when we're having games in the afternoon. Maybe Uncle Harry could teach you a few of my skills, too, Ryan."

"That would really be fun, but with having to go to school every day, it might be hard to come. Maybe on one of our school break days or vacation time, I'll ask Mom if I can do that," Ryan told his Uncle.

A knock came to the door. "That sounds like Mom; I'll get the door," Ryan said. Ryan opened the door and saw his mother standing there. "Hi, Mom. Do we have to go home now?"

"Yes, Ryan; your dad is waiting out in the truck," Joanne said. "Your room looks pretty good now, Uncle Harry. I'm so glad we went shopping that day to buy you a new chair."

"Thanks, Joanne, and do come again soon. Thanks for leaving Ryan with me for a couple of hours this evening; I sure enjoyed his visit."

Harry soon settled for the evening. He wondered what Joanne and Ted had to say about seeing Amelia and him in the café. *Maybe that was better than finding us in the new Look Out Café. Little do they know, we've been together there, too. Sounds to me like they had quite a time looking for Harry.*

16 HANNAH'S *New* POSITION

With the help of her family and some of their friends, Hannah moved into her new home. She settled in fairly well, but was soon thinking about her upcoming first day of work. She found the neighbours to be friendly and very helpful. One lady who lived just two doors away came by with fresh homemade muffins the second day after the major move. Hannah felt a welcome for sure to Elm Valley, Saskatchewan. The house she bought was about three blocks from work. On a nice day, she'd enjoy the walk to Home Acres Retirement Home.

Hannah headed off to work on the first Tuesday in August. It was a bright, sunny day. She chose to drive her van, as she was sensing a little nervousness that first day. She wore a royal blue suit and dress shoes. As her interview was in July, she had a fairly confident feeling of where to find Elaine Agnew's D.O.N.'s office. She definitely was headed in that direction as she entered Hope Acres at 8:30 a.m. on her first day.

"Good morning, Hannah, and welcome to Hope Acres," Elaine Agnew greeted her. "I'm sure you're exhausted after house hunting and the move. How did everything go for you?"

"Actually, everything seemed to fall in place. My whole family came to Elm Valley a few weeks ago, and we found suitable housing. Then my son and son-in-law organized the big move, and I felt things worked out quite well," Hannah answered. "One amazing thing happened as we were all sitting in the Look Out Café. Jerrad's cell phone rang just before we went up to the real estate office. Of all places to receive a call regarding his application for a new position at the John Deere Company in Manitoba. He'd been waiting several weeks for this call. Everyone was excited to learn that he'd been accepted for the position. I'm sure that restaurant wondered what all the excitement was about on that Saturday afternoon."

"I can just imagine," Elaine said. "In this fairly small community, everyone wants to know just what's going on. And this would definitely be a timely call for your family to receive." Mrs. Agnew found it very special for Hannah to share this happy news.

"I want you to make yourself at home today. Feel free to just walk around the various areas of care. Before I forget, I do have a name tag for you to wear, just to help the staff to get acquainted with you. And by the way, do feel comfortable just calling me Elaine. I'd like that," Elaine told her.

Hannah wondered just how her new job would be organized, but she knew that the D.O.N. would certainly guide her along. She listened carefully and took down some notes as Elaine told her about a few events that would be coming up. She gave her a copy of the July calendar outlining the various plans for the residents.

"You need to mark this Friday in your day timer. We're holding a special welcome dinner for you. It will be held in the conference room. You'll meet the ladies and gentleman who head up the various departments in our facility. A few of the county members have been invited as well," Elaine informed Hannah.

"How nice is this! I'll certainly mark that down in my day timer right away. Thanks so much," Hannah expressed.

Before the D.O.N. gave her the free time to just walk around the facility and chat with people along the way, she gave Hannah a folder and calendar of events, with slots that she would no doubt be working on. She assured Hannah that she would indeed be assisting her in these first few months, and they would work on these monthly calendars together.

At around l0:00 a.m. Hannah started out on her get-acquainted walk throughout the building. She kept wondering if she would recognize anyone from years ago, and if anyone would recognize her after all these years. She walked by the room where the staff were doing exercises with the residents. Most of the residents were in wheelchairs, and it looked like the staff were doing very good arm and hand exercises with them. One of the staff greeted Hannah.

"Good morning! You must be the new staff member we've been hearing about. Welcome to Hope Acres. It's coffee time for us after we get these residents back to the lounge areas. You're welcome to join us in the café," Betty said.

"Thank you. Perhaps I'll just speak to a few residents sitting in the lounge area, and then I'll watch for you so I can join you in the café," Hannah said. She felt welcomed already by the nursing staff.

Hannah was slowly finding her way around when she came to a lounge with a gentleman sitting in a comfortable chair. She looked at him and shook his hand to greet him.

"Harry Jones! What are you doing here?"

"Are you Hannah?" Harry asked as he stood up.

"Yes, and this is my first day of work here. I thought I'd just walk around and greet a few people. I wondered if I would meet anyone I knew. I can't believe this! You and I were in the same graduating class in high school. Don't ask me how many years ago that was," Hannah said.

"I heard about a new staff person coming, but I had no idea who it would be," Harry said.

"Harry, I do need to talk with you longer at another time. It will be a very busy first week for me, but don't you worry—I'll see you one of these days, and we'll catch up on old times."

Hannah followed along with Betty as she saw her coming towards the café. Lori, her co-worker, was with her.

"So, Mrs. Jensen, I understand you came here from Manitoba. We never had an Activity Director in our old building. We're sure happy to welcome you here," said Lori.

"Thank you, girls, for your very nice welcome. It's going to take me days to get know the nursing staff, not to mention all these residents.

Tell me about Elm Valley; it's been years since I lived here. My sister, Helen, and I moved with our parents when they decided to move back to Manitoba," Hannah shared while sipping on her coffee.

"Well, we don't have a lot of time right now, but we can tell you that the big event the town has been working on for weeks now is our Elm Valley Fall Fair to take place on September 9 and 10 in the community centre and fair grounds. Quite a few residents will definitely be interested in attending some of the events. I think last year some of them even put some craft entries in and were excited about seeing if they won a prize," Betty shared.

"Thanks! I wasn't expecting to get information like this so soon on my job. You girls enjoy your day, and I'm sure we'll be meeting together soon. I do plan to have several meetings with the nursing staff," Hannah said as she left the café to continue her walk around.

Hannah wanted to greet the staff and residents in the locked in area. When she worked at Prairie Lane Nursing Home, she felt it very rewarding when her shifts were in this type of setting. She asked one of the housekeeping staff along the way what the code would be to get into the locked unit.

"Good morning," she said to a couple of staff members who were waiting for someone to come back from coffee break so they could leave for theirs.

"Good morning! You must be Mrs. Jensen. We were told about you starting your new position today."

"Just call me Hannah. I lived here years ago. I just met a fellow who used to be in the same class as me at high school. I wonder who else I might possibly recognize."

"So what brings you back to Saskatchewan after all these years?" one of the staff asked.

"Well, I had an activity director's job at a facility called Prairie Lane Nursing Home. Then one day, the county came for their meeting with department heads. I was informed that my position was being terminated, as the county was doing cutbacks. I was devastated! Actually, it all happened the very weekend of my mother's eightieth birthday party. I really hadn't felt like retiring yet, although I know a lot of people who would at my age. To make a long story short, my daughter, Jen, looked on the Internet to see if there were jobs available in Manitoba for activity directors, but there was nothing. Then she noticed an ad for a brand new facility in Elm Valley. I applied, and here I am!"

"We sure welcome you here, and all best in this new position, Mrs. Jensen," the staff member said.

Hannah walked around in the locked area, shaking hands and sometimes sitting down at the residents' level and chatting with them. She greeted them with smiles, and some of them smiled back. Her thoughts went back to Prairie Lane Nursing Home, where she still missed the staff and residents.

It was getting close to lunch time. Hannah made her way back to the D.O.N.'s office. They'd set up a meeting for 1:30 p.m. Hannah arrived back after lunch and made her way to the meeting. She shared briefly about her walk around the facility.

"I never covered all the areas I thought I would, but there is always another day," Hannah commented.

"One of the major items I want to discuss, Hannah, is something we touched on briefly at the time of your interview. In our old building, we didn't work very hard at getting volunteers for our facility. I think we both agreed that we want to definitely work on this," Mrs. Agnew said.

Hannah was very pleased that this was on the D.O.N.'s agenda.

"I thought of different ways we could do this. We could definitely put a notice in the *Elm Valley Herald*," Elaine said. "What suggestions do you have regarding this idea of recruiting some volunteers, Hannah?"

"I was thinking that if a small table was placed near the front entrance, we could set up a poster and brief letters and questionnaires for interested volunteers to pick up and take home. The letter would ask them to bring the forms to our meeting for the volunteers," Hannah suggested.

"This sounds like a very good idea, and our secretary, Mary, could certainly give us a hand in making the posters," Elaine commented.

"We could also contact the community churches; I'm sure there must be several people who would be interested in becoming a volunteer," Hannah added.

"We'll get back to this on another day, Hannah; I can see that your heart is sure into this great idea of having a volunteer program. I'm sure you are already thinking of having a volunteer Christmas event, too. It gets so busy during the Christmas season, so we definitely would plan this near the latter part of November," Elaine expressed.

"You've got that right! It's exactly how I've been thinking. Thanks, Elaine, for taking time for this first meeting together. I've enjoyed my first day, for sure!"

Hannah drove to her new home, thankful for the first day at work. She relaxed for the evening and went over her notes from the meeting with the D.O.N. She did promise she would give Jen a call and tell her how she got through this first day at her new position.

That night, Hannah wrote in her journal about her new position and the highlights of her first day.

What I enjoyed most about my first day was the walk around the facility meeting staff and residents and stopping in at the locked area. I felt good about shaking hands with some of the residents and sitting at their level while they were sitting in lounge chairs or wheelchairs. Noticing Harry Jones in the main lounge was the big surprise of my first day.

17 HARRY'S *First Official* DATE

Amelia was wondering when Harry would give her the promised call. She was almost ready to retire after her ten years of working as a Red Cross homemaker. Her last scheduled booking was only one week away. She was relaxing after her trying day of getting all the work done for her client—the one who always made her a long list of duties. Her telephone rang, and she quickly reached over to answer the call.

"Hello, Amelia, this is Harry speaking."

"Good to hear your voice, Harry. I just knew you wouldn't forget your promise. You're no doubt relieved that the auction is over," Amelia said.

"I sure am. It was such a busy time, but I did notice you working at the food booth," Harry commented.

"The church ladies were short of help and asked me give them a hand. Talk about busy! Everyone seemed to have a real social time, and they so enjoyed the food we served," Amelia told Harry.

"Thanks for all your work at the lunch booth. I finally did have a piece of pie near the end of the auction. It certainly was a hectic day, to say the least," Harry said. "Did you hear about Ryan raising his hand a few times to bid. I know Joanne was quite nervous about him bidding on the antique car. He didn't get it, but he sure raised the bids a little higher each time he put his hand up. I'm just wondering, Amelia … are you free this coming Saturday?"

"Yes, Harry. I try to keep my weekends free," Amelia replied.

"Would you like to go to a movie over in the next town, and then go out for dinner to a restaurant?" Harry questioned.

"Yes, I would be very happy to go with you. It would feel like an early retirement celebration, as I only have one week left to go," Amelia responded.

"Since we have to drive those extra miles, I'll come by and pick you up at 1:00 p.m. I'm really glad you can go with me. I'll see you on Saturday. Bye for now." Harry put the receiver down carefully and released a big breath.

The days seemed long waiting for the weekend and thinking about his outing with Amelia on Saturday. When Saturday finally arrived, Harry remembered to sign out after lunch and told the R.P.N. on duty that he wouldn't be at dinner that evening. He drove a few blocks to where Amelia lived. She was right ready for the evening. Harry got out of his truck and opened the door for Amelia.

"I like your new summer jacket, Harry; it looks good on you," Amelia said as they drove off in the truck.

"Thanks, Amelia. You're looking very nice all dressed up this evening; usually I just see you in your Red Cross uniform," Harry said.

"Thanks. It sure feels great to dress up this evening for our outing." Then she continued. "Harry, I must thank you again for that generous amount of money you gave me for doing those two last shifts with you. I needed to buy something new, so I went to that big clothing store in town and purchased this new outfit I'm wearing today. My new friend, Jill, the store clerk, assisted me in choosing it."

They drove around town and found the movie theatre. Harry parked his truck, and they walked toward the theatre. They picked up a bag of freshly popped popcorn and found good seats about half way up. They chatted all through the advertising part. It had been years since Harry had been to a theatre. During the western movie, Harry reached over and took Amelia's hand. She looked at him and smiled.

After the movie, Harry and Amelia drove around the town. Much to their delight, they found a restaurant advertising a "Buffet Evening."

"Perfect," Harry said.

They found a parking spot and walked into the restaurant. The friendly waiter found them a nice booth. Such an array of food! They both thoroughly enjoyed their favourite types of food on the buffet tables. During the meal, they had lots of time to share together. Harry talked about the auction and the new owners coming to the farm very soon. He talked about Joanne and Ryan coming to Hope Acres, and the trouble they had finding him. Amelia found this quite amusing. Of course, she had heard the story before about the morning Sam and Harry went apartment hunting.

"Harry," Amelia said, "you could write a book about all the visits with your niece and how she never phoned ahead of time."

"I guess it's dessert time for us, Amelia. You know how I always look forward to this, and no doubt there will be so many different kinds this evening."

While they were enjoying their desserts and coffee, Amelia shared about one of her homemaking experiences. She was assisting a lady with her weekly bath; she was quite a big lady. Even with the handles on the tub, there was no way Amelia could help her out without hurting herself. So, she had to call for help.

"It wasn't in Elm Valley," she explained, "but another town. So, like they taught us in our course, I had to call the fire department. Of course, I let the water out of the tub and wrapped her in towels to keep her warm. She was so embarrassed; you can be sure she had one of those chairs put in the tub very soon."

"And what does your story remind me of, Amelia?" Harry smiled. "I'll never forget how helpless I felt on the barn floor, and how you had to send for help for me. Then when we got back to the farm, people kept calling to ask if we had a fire on the farm. I'll always remember that."

Amelia chatted a bit about Hope Acres advertising in the local newspaper for volunteers.

"You would make a wonderful volunteer!" Harry said encouragingly. "Oh, I almost forgot to tell you. I had a quite the experience last week. It was after breakfast, and I was just sitting in the lounge area. A very nice looking lady all dressed up was walking around and came to say hello. Before she got to introducing herself, she said, 'Harry Jones, what are you doing here? I can't believe this!'" He explained that he and Hannah had been in the same high school graduating class, and now she was the new Activity Director.

"So, Amelia, can I get you a cup of tea before we leave the restaurant and head back to Elm Valley?"

"Thanks, Harry, but I've really enjoyed this buffet, and I won't bother having any more tea right now. It's been a wonderful evening with you," Amelia expressed.

Harry and Amelia headed to the parking lot, and he opened the door for her to get into the truck. They chatted in the truck for awhile, and then Harry walked Amelia to the door.

"Thanks again for the very nice evening, Amelia."

"This has been like a celebration, as this week marks ten years at my position with the Red Cross," Amelia said. "You must feel the same way, as your auction is over and you're moved into Hope Acres. Thanks kindly for this celebration evening!"

"More than that, Amelia," Harry continued, "I feel comfortable with you. We'll be talking and planning more events together—you can be sure of that."

18 HANNAH'S *Plans for* THE VOLUNTEERS

Harry Jones sat by himself in the café on Monday morning. It was Hannah's second week of work. She remembered that she promised him she would have a chat with him. It was about 10:00 a.m., and she had a few minutes before she had a meeting with the D.O.N.

"Good morning, Harry! I finally found a few moments to sit down and have a little chat with you. I hope you're settling in quite nicely in this new facility," Hannah greeted. She sat at a table with Harry and picked up a glass of juice from the machine in the café.

Harry told her that he was slowly getting adjusted, and that he was looking forward to the first games afternoon.

"Do I remember correctly that you enjoy playing chess and other games?" Hannah asked.

"Yes, and my good neighbour, Sam, plans to come up sometime this week and have a game with me. Both of us recently joined a community crokinole club for both the young and old. If you wish, Hannah, I could bring my board to your games day sometime."

"Thanks for sharing this, Harry. I'm sure you'll be a big help to me. Right now I feel I can use all the help that comes my way," Hannah said. "Harry, I really need to talk with you and share something that has been on my heart and mind. I wanted to tell you that my mother passed away several weeks after the family celebrated her eightieth birthday. My sister, Helen, and I had the big job of cleaning out her house and going through a lot of papers and items. I'm sure you'll know what a big job this is, as you've just been through all that. I have to tell you this, as it really bothered me when Helen told me that when she was going through papers in our mother's desk, she found a letter that was addressed to me. It was still sealed, or perhaps opened and sealed again. I felt so badly when Helen showed me the note, which was from you. How kind of you to invite me to go with you to our high school prom! To think that I never answered it really bothered me. I do apologize, even though this happened many years ago."

Harry hardly knew what to say. "I'm really glad you told me, Hannah. Over the years, I often wondered where my letter got to. I used to think of it as the lost note. Thank you so much for telling me your story. When you do have a little more time, it would be fun to talk about our good old high school days. It's a small world, especially when you meet friends again after so many years," Harry said with his hand trembling a little as he hung onto his cane.

Later that day, Hannah worked on filling in the residents' calendar for September and October. She felt overwhelmed, especially by trying to set up a volunteer program. She worried about how to work things out the best way as she slowly learned to take one step at a time.

Eventually, the volunteer program was set up and the posters were ready for the churches and community organizations in the area. The special meeting for those interested in being a volunteer was set for September 22 at 1:00 p.m. in the chapel.

Hannah chose to attend the Community Church after she got settled into her new home. She was impressed with their welcome and smiling faces.

There was a ladies' group in Elm Valley called the Friendship Bible Study. They meet in the Community Seniors' Centre. The group was discussing the need for some kind of a project during the Christmas season. It just so happened that Doreen, the group leader, had received several copies of the advertising for the volunteers' program at Hope Acres Retirement Home. There was some discussion, and Dayle spoke up.

"Maybe Mrs. Jensen would have something she would need some help with regarding the organization of the volunteers."

"Would you like to give her a call and see if there is something our group could help with near the Christmas season?" Doreen suggested to Dayle.

The very next week, Dayle had the answer. The new Activity Director told her that on November 23 she was planning a Christmas Appreciation Tea for the volunteers. The Friendship Bible Study group got excited, and Barb said, "This is exactly something we could help with."

"Mrs. Jensen will give us more information soon," Dayle continued, "and she'll purchase the materials to make the little Christmas bags from the cotton Christmas fabric. She'll also provide the items for the Christmas bags for the volunteers. She'll need some old Christmas cards. She has a poem to be printed out and placed on the Christmas card that will somehow be attached to the little gift bags. The ladies continued with their study time after deciding that someone in the group would be in touch with the new Activity Director at Hope Acres.

Hannah arrived home from her very busy day and brought her files home with her. She so appreciated the call from one of the ladies from the Friendship Bible Study Group. Dayle had called just when she was feeling overwhelmed with all that she had to do. As Hannah was relaxing and finding something for her supper, she had a feeling that God was with her. She realized that when she felt most pressured, He sent her creative ideas and help along the way. There were times that she thought about her life and how her family seemed to be there for her. In difficult times, she thought of her husband, Nick, and how he had an accident at work and then the heart attack later that took his life just five years ago.

The volunteer program had been a great success, and the meeting for the volunteers brought about thirty-five people to Hope Acres. Some of them chose just to be available for special events. Others wanted to have a specific resident to do one on one visits with. Hannah was happy to see some gentlemen join as well. There was such a need for gentlemen to come and visit a specific resident.

Hannah contacted the new crokinole club in town and told them the date for a games afternoon. She asked if there would be four or five people willing to come to the large recreation gym where the card tables and games would be set up. She thanked them all individually for coming and assisting. So many knew how to play this game years ago, and they seemed very pleased with the fun time they enjoyed that afternoon. She made an announcement about the Christmas Volunteer Appreciation Tea to be held on November 23 from 2:00 to 4:00 p.m. She invited them to join them on that afternoon.

Hannah found that the time flew by in her new position. At Thanksgiving, she invited her whole family to come to Elm Valley to enjoy a turkey dinner and all the trimmings. She felt so good about doing this, and they all had lots of questions about how she was coping with her big job. Jen and Holly wanted to bring the desserts, and she certainly didn't refuse their offer. Maddison and Tim couldn't wait until Nana would take them up to the café in the new facility. The family also gave her some ideas for the Christmas Tea.

"Be sure and check out the community and see if there is a children's choir available," Jen suggested. "That would be great entertainment for the folks."

"Thanks, Jen, for this suggestion. I want to keep the program short, but with time right at the end for singing some Christmas carols. Then we'll have our tea time and Christmas treats for everyone. I'll work right away on your suggestion about a children's choir."

Hannah told her family about the community Bible study group, and how they wanted to help with a Christmas project.

"I never refuse offers to help," she said, "so I have them all booked up to do some favours for the volunteers."

"That's wonderful, Mom," Holly said. "This will be so helpful to you, and it will make them feel so good about doing these Christmas favours for the volunteers."

Jerrad and John asked if they were going to be the guest singers.

"Sorry, fellows," Hannah laughed, "but if you show up, I have a special job for you."

"What would that be, Mom?" Jerrad asked.

"Well, we can always use some very special clean up fellows," Hannah said jokingly.

The weeks passed by and soon the Christmas season was fast approaching. Jen called her mom on November 23 in the evening. She knew it had been the day of the Christmas Volunteers Appreciation Tea.

"Hi, Mom! Just calling as I can't wait to hear how you made out at the Christmas Volunteers Appreciation Tea this afternoon," Jen greeted.

"Jen, everything went really well," Hannah said. "It was well attended, and the volunteers seemed to really enjoy the afternoon. And, by the way, the community has a children's choir; they go to special events, especially at Christmas. Thanks for that great idea! I could tell that the residents really enjoyed the children singing the Christmas songs. The singing of the carols was very special. I want to tell you that the most wonderful thing happened regarding the carol sing. I wasn't sure what we would do, as the lady who was to play the piano for the carols didn't show up. Gloria, one of our volunteers, chose a resident from the locked area. Her name is Ginger. She always loved playing the piano, and she even gave music lessons a few years ago and was the church pianist in her community church. Sometimes when Gloria would come to visit she couldn't find Ginger in her room. She would ask around, and sure enough, someone would say, 'I took her to the chapel; you'll find her sitting by the piano, or she might even be playing the piano.' This afternoon, her husband, Harold, brought her from her unit. She looked so pretty in her new pretty, blue coloured pantsuit that her husband purchased for her. The hairdresser in Hope Acres washed and set her hair that morning. Gloria told Harold that she didn't mind sitting with Ginger in the front row near the piano. Ginger's husband sat in the third row back. Everyone was waiting to see what would happen with the carol singing with no pianist. Gloria gently got Ginger to stand, and she took her hand and helped her to sit at the piano. Ginger smiled.

"I announced that the first carol would be 'O Come all ye Faithful.' Ginger struck the first note, and that's all it took. She did amazingly well! I then announced 'O Little Town of Bethlehem' and closed with 'Silent Night.' Gloria looked over at Ginger's husband; he was smiling. Everyone who could stood up and heartedly clapped for Ginger! In response, Ginger turned toward everyone with a smile and said, 'For the moment, I remembered!'

"Jen, since I've started my new position, this experience is my most rewarding one. To see Ginger filling in for someone else, and do such a great job, was so wonderful. I wasn't the only one with tears in my eyes. The volunteers enjoyed their Christmas gifts made by the ladies of the Friendship Bible Study Group, and everyone enjoyed the Christmas cookies and tea. I'm sorry I kept you on the phone so long!" Hannah said as she looked at the clock.

"Mom, I enjoyed every minute of it. I could just picture myself being there. I'm so happy that everyone enjoyed it, and that you enjoyed the children's choir. I agree that it must have been so rewarding for you to see Ginger, a resident who had to go into a facility because of her loss of memory, do what she did today. I can just picture her playing the piano for the carols, and you as you led the carol singing. Good job, Mom!"

Hannah went home that evening from Hope Acres Retirement and Nursing Home with a sense of gratitude toward the facility for hiring her. She felt rewarded in a way that was hard to express. Although she had many challenges ahead of her, she was grateful for all the nursing staff, the housekeeping staff, office staff, and other employees who had a part in her life at the new facility. She felt so proud to be a part of the community of Elm Valley in Saskatchewan.

19 *Amelia* AND HARRY

Christmas was soon approaching, and Amelia was getting ready for the festive season. She and Harry seemed to be going on regular date nights ever since their official first date a couple of months ago when they enjoyed their buffet dinner together out of town. One Saturday evening Harry's phone rang.

"Just wondering if you'd be interested in attending the Community Church tomorrow," Amelia asked. "The service begins at 10:30 a.m."

There was some silence, and then Harry said, "That might be a good idea. So many of those people helped me with the auction, and maybe I've put this off long enough. I'd like to pick you up, as I wouldn't feel comfortable going on my own."

"This is good news! I'll be ready to go shortly after 10:00 a.m."

"You know me … I'll be right on time. I'll see you in the morning. Bye for now, Amelia."

Harry knew one thing—he certainly was prepared to have a suit to wear, after that big shopping trip when he lost Collie for a while. He would never forget that one. He felt honoured that Amelia would phone and ask him to go with her. *It's one thing to start reading my Bible; now I'm going to church*! He wondered just how he would enjoy the service.

On Sunday morning, Harry kept his promise and picked up Amelia. They found a good parking spot, as they were a little early for the service. When they walked into church together, Jake, the pastor's son greeted them with a big smile.

"Good morning, young fellow," Harry said.

"Our church is welcoming all ages," Amelia said to Harry, "and lately they're training the youth to be greeters and also ushers."

They found a seat four rows from the back of the sanctuary. Pastor Phil welcomed them with a handshake.

"Good to see you, Mr. Jones, and you too, Amelia."

There was still about five minutes before the service was to start. Sam and Ellen came in just after Harry and Amelia. They sat across the aisle and a little further up. Ellen gave a quiet message to Sam, who then came over to the pew were Harry and Amelia were sitting.

"Ellen said to tell you that she put a roast in the oven and wondered if you both could join us for dinner after the service," Sam invited.

Amelia whispered the message to Harry. He replied, "It's up to you, Amelia; I would gladly accept this invitation."

"Yes, Sam, we're happy to accept your invitation for dinner today," Amelia said quietly.

The service was soon to start, and the song leader welcomed everyone and then opened the service with prayer. Amelia whispered to Harry, "If you find you can't stand for all the hymns, feel free to be seated."

Pastor Phil's message was titled, "Why Worry When You Can Pray?" He encouraged the congregation with the Bible verses found in Philippians 4:6–7. After the church service, Harry was impressed by how friendly the people were. A lot of them knew Amelia, as she has been going for quite a while this past year. Some even mentioned the auction to Harry, which was weeks ago now.

Ellen and Sam made Amelia and Harry feel very welcome in their home. As Ellen had more preparations to do, Sam entertained Amelia and Harry in the living room.

"So, Harry, tell us about your life at Hope Acres Retirement Home," Sam asked.

"I've been there a good three months now. It isn't as boring as I thought it would be. For a while, it was hard to keep remembering to sign out and sign back in. Today, though, I did sign out after breakfast, as I knew I was going out to church. I guess you heard about the time Ryan's parents came and tried to find me. They had the nurses trying to locate me, and even checked with the dietary staff to see if I did sign out. I hadn't gone anywhere that day."

"No, Harry, I didn't hear that story," Sam replied.

"Well, Ryan's parents came to Elm Valley in the afternoon, and they wanted to leave Ryan for a while to visit with me. My good friend, Amelia here, came to the facility and spent an hour with her resident that she is involved with through the volunteer program. Then she and I planned to meet in the café around 3:00 p.m. That's where they finally found us; Amelia did a great job of making them welcome and got them tea and juice and offered them cookies."

"Okay, everyone, you can all sit in now; dinner is finally all ready," Ellen said to her guests. She asked Sam to say a blessing on the meal.

"Thank you for inviting us. Imagine, going to church on my first Sunday and getting an invitation out for dinner," Harry expressed.

"You are most welcome! We've been wanting to have you both in for a meal for some time now, especially since Amelia just retired. Harry, you've had so much to do on the farm, there just didn't seem to be any end to the work for quite a while," Ellen said.

"You know, folks, I feel that it's a brand new world for me now. Amelia and I have known one another ever since she became my Red Cross homemaker. We were always both so busy with our responsibilities."

"And now you can spend time with one another, and I know you're enjoying one another's company," Sam offered.

"Is everyone ready for a cup of tea now and some dessert?" Ellen asked.

"We sure are, Ellen, and I think I'm saying this for our guests, too."

"Ellen, can I help to clear these plates for you?" Amelia asked. "It's my line of duty, you know."

"Sure, Amelia. I'll get the cups and take care of the tea, and I hope everyone likes peach pie with whipped cream."

The four friends were soon enjoying a wonderful dessert. "This pie is delicious, Ellen! We sure don't see pie too often up at Hope Acres," Harry said.

They all relaxed in the living room for a while, and Ellen was firm about not doing the dishes right away.

"I have a question for both of you," Sam began, "but first let me tell you that this coming weekend, the seniors in our community are booking a bus trip for the day. I'm not really involved, but I read the ad in the *Elm Valley Herald* recently. Since it is the Christmas season, the seniors are taking a bus trip to the town next to us—about forty-five minutes from here. When you live on the prairies, it never seems very far. They have a theatre group with local talent that performs plays. This play is to be a Christmas comedy. I think the bus is leaving at 9:00 a.m. We can shop a little, and everyone buys their own lunch. The comedy begins at 2:00 p.m. Is this something that you two might be interested in going to next Saturday? We need to decide fairly soon, as the bus can fill up pretty quickly. I know it's a very busy season."

Amelia spoke up first. "I think it would be fun to go and see a play put on by local talent in the community nearby."

"What about you, Harry?" Sam asked.

"Seems lately, I'm game for anything; sure, I'd like to go next Saturday," Harry said.

"Since tomorrow is Monday, would it be okay if I contact the person involved with taking names of those interested?" Sam inquired.

"We would really appreciate this, Sam and Ellen. If there is still room for Harry and me, just give me a call," Amelia suggested. "Perhaps it's time for Harry and I to leave after a wonderful afternoon. Harry has to get back to sign in. I hope no one was looking for him this evening."

Harry thanked his good neighbours for the delicious meal and very nice visit, and Amelia commented on how much she enjoyed the meal and wonderful visit, too.

On the way home, Harry and Amelia talked about their day.

"Harry, I've so enjoyed you coming to church with me, and then when Sam and Ellen invited us for dinner, it just seemed to add a huge plus to our day," Amelia said.

"Thanks, Amelia. I think this has been a very wonderful day in my life, too," Harry replied. "Let me know when you're coming up to Hope Acres this week. By then we might know the plans for next Saturday. It would be nice to go on that seniors' bus trip to see the Christmas comedy and do a little shopping," Harry commented before he said goodbye to Amelia.

Christmas was fast approaching, and the snow was piling up on the prairies. Amelia was making plans for her Christmas dinner; she had already invited Harry to come, along with a couple of her cousins who lived in the community. They each lived alone.

The weekend of the Christmas comedy was very successful. A full busload enjoyed a wonderful day away, and Amelia and Harry, along with Sam and Ellen, really had a great time. Harry even had a little time to do some shopping when the ladies were looking in a ladies' clothing store.

20 *Christmas* EVE

Harry noticed an advertisement regarding a Christmas buffet on Christmas Eve from 4:30 p.m. to 6:30 p.m. Anyone interested was to call and book either for 4:30 p.m. or 6:30 p.m. Harry talked with Amelia, and they chose the 4:30 p.m. sitting, as the weather forecast was calling for more snow and very cold temperatures. They wouldn't have to go out of town, as the buffet was advertised for the local Look Out Café.

Harry was in agreement with Amelia's plans for Christmas. The two love birds would be celebrating their first Christmas together. Amelia really struggled over what to get Harry for Christmas. She felt there wasn't much he needed, living in one room at Hope Acres. She thought about getting him something for his new truck.

Harry sure knew what his gift would be for Amelia. He dressed up nicely for the Christmas Eve buffet, as he knew Amelia would be decked out in the new outfit she bought that past week when they went on the seniors' bus trip.

It seemed a long day for both of them as they waited for their first Christmas Eve outing together. Harry decided to purchase some roses. He took them to the Look Out Café the day before the buffet, so that the waiter or waitress would bring them to the table as a surprise for Amelia.

Harry picked Amelia up shortly after 4:00 p.m., so they wouldn't have to rush. Just as he thought, she was wearing her beautiful new outfit, along with a dazzling necklace, silver bracelet, and high heels.

"You look so nice in your new outfit, Amelia," Harry complimented.

The parking lot at the café had been plowed that day, so there was no problem getting a parking place. The temperature was fifteen degrees below zero, but it was a nice, clear evening.

Amelia and Harry seemed to always arrive early. They got a nice booth, and the waiting time was quite relaxing. The restaurant filled up quite quickly, and they did see quite a few familiar faces. The Look Out Café was nicely decorated, and the Christmas tree was beautiful with a gold star on top. The buffet featured a full turkey dinner with all the trimmings and a great variety of salads. They enjoyed a lot of different salads first and took their time enjoying their turkey dinner. There were several waitresses and one male waiter on duty. They came around to fill their glasses with ice water and serve the tea and coffee at various times.

Dessert time, of course, was the best part of the meal. Amelia noticed that Harry seemed a little nervous. She wasn't sure why, as everyone in the restaurant was talking and laughing and having a great time. They went to the buffet table and picked up small servings of various desserts and berries. When they sat down, the friendly waiter came to offer tea.

Amelia asked for tea, but when the waiter went to pour it in her cup, he said, "Oh, I guess I better not use that one." Amelia looked in her cup and saw a piece of paper and a chocolate. She pulled out the piece of paper, which was shaped like a red-trimmed heart. On the note was written, "WILL YOU MARRY ME?"

"Oh, Harry, my answer is yes!" She reached over and gave him a hug and a kiss.

Harry sat smiling as the waiter rushed away to bring the bouquet of roses that Harry had left the day before with his instructions. He set the roses on their table.

"I'm not sure I can handle all this excitement," Amelia said. "These roses are beautiful, Harry. Thank you so much!"

The waiter came with the tea. "Are you both ready now for your tea?" he asked as he served each of them a cup of tea.

Harry reached into his pocket and pulled out a small package done up in blue paper with a silver bow on top. He gave it to Amelia. She opened up the box. Her face lit up, and her eyes were filled with tears of joy.

"Oh, Harry, thank you! It's so beautiful." She continued to hold the engagement ring in her hand. The guests didn't realize that they were in for some entertainment at the Look Out Café that evening. Several guests near their booth stood up and clapped for Harry and Amelia. Harry stood up to say a few words.

"Thank you kindly," he began. "You better see if this ring fits you, Amelia. I just guessed at the right size for you."

"It's perfect, Harry," Amelia said with a big smile.

The time was getting closer to the next setting for the buffet, but the waiter came by and told the couple that there had been a few cancellations, so they could stay at their table as long as they liked. Harry and Amelia were happy to linger a little longer. They began to discuss the wedding; Harry asked if an early spring wedding would be okay. Amelia readily agreed with his suggestion. They decided that they still had lots of time to think about the honeymoon.

"You totally surprised me this evening, Harry," Amelia said. "Now I know why you were anxious to get that little shopping trip in last weekend when we went out of town on the bus trip. Little did I know what you were anxious to purchase that day."

"No problem, Amelia. I felt that this evening was just the right time to have this little celebration," Harry said as he picked up the bill for the buffet and left an extra big tip.

"Thanks, Harry. This has been the most wonderful evening, and it's just the beginning of you and I enjoying a great relationship together."

As they walked out to the car, Amelia suddenly exclaimed, "I just remembered something! The Community Church is having their Christmas Eve service at 8:00 p.m."

"Did you want to attend that, Amelia?" asked Harry.

"Actually, Harry, we really don't have to. Tomorrow is Christmas, and we'll be celebrating with my cousins. And we celebrated our wonderful event this Christmas Eve. Harry, why don't I take my flowers home and set them on my dining room table, and then we can take a nice drive around the community and look at all the Christmas lights. I really haven't taken time all these busy days to even do this."

"Good idea, Amelia! I would be quite happy to have a relaxing evening after that delicious buffet we enjoyed."

Amelia and Harry enjoyed the most wonderful Christmas Eve together, and when the buds and blossoms come out in the spring, they'll have their quiet wedding just as they planned. And who knows ... maybe the old Hope Acres Nursing Home might have that facility all changed into seniors' apartments.